Dandelion

Dandelion

A story of Courage

Audrey Louise Shanahan

2011

Dedication

To the guy I share my life with and who knows who he is, I say thank you. You once sent me a note I'll never forget: "If one dream should fall and break into a thousand different pieces, never be afraid to pick up one of those pieces and begin again." I don't know where you stole the words from, but I know how you knew how much I needed to hear them at the time. I love that you always know and care about what I need. What can I say only that I feel lucky to be splitting my rent with you.

To my best friend, Julie: we have a connection neither of us really understands. All we know is that it's a little bit special. You're my comfort when it all gets a bit tough and my partner in crime when times are good. Thank you for being you.

To the innumerable teachers and helpers I have had in this life, from the wisdom of Jac O'Keefe to the wonderful frivolity of my Team Journo crew in London. To the friends I made in Vietnam, especially jealous chili, who knows who she is and why I love her.

To Dee: another soul with whom I share an unbreakable connection. I have wanted to share my journey with you ever since you dared me to run down that cliff face in Pinewood Forest all those years ago. You continue to push my boundaries in the most loving way. We're for siempre.

To Deepa, Emily, Ruth and Jack — the latter two for making my belly ache with the best sort of pain and the former two for being a constant source of inspiration and security.

To the people who read early drafts of the book, like Isabel, Laura and Fiona. Thanks, gals! You all rock and you know it!!

To life-fixer extraordinaire, Pat Neville, for being a champion motivator.

To my granny, Dolly Lynch, for taking a gamble on me. I hope it paid off.

And lastly, but most importantly, the Shanahans from Tola Park. I would be lost without my big fat family! I love every one of you and want to thank you for always being there for me and always believing in me.

I.

A pink feathered August twilight turned to night. Lillian took a deep breath in and held it, suspended, until she absorbed every atom of the twinkling sky. Its frequency switched hers to almost still, like rain water drip-dropping on a summer leaf. It was time to sleep. But before her journey to sub-conscious-ness, one last spectacle auditioned for attention. Golden thought bubbles often came in gentle showers, as nourishment from the highest floor of her fantasy-prone mind. Tonight, a single orb floated alone, bright and growing brighter. It flickered into a wish that some day the man lying asleep on the other side of the bed would ask her to be his wife. Her full lips stretched in a smile as it prophesised her wedding day. Nothing was sweeter than night-dreaming.

Then out of nothing, there was a movement—not hers and not Phil's. Her instincts screamed danger. She sat up, adrenaline pumping. They weren't alone. Thumps from her heart flooded her ears, turning her blood cold. *What was that noise?* she asked herself, too terrified to attempt an answer.

A silhouette darted across the balcony; a man, a burglar, in black, with a weapon. Her voice left her, like the worst kind of traitor; the kind that leaves in an hour of need. Alone, she tried desperately to cope with the terrifying realisa-tion that someone was trying to get into their home. Her arms and legs joined the mutiny, freezing her to the bed. Gloved fingers from outside separated the curtains. The intruder walked through and looked straight into her eyes through the slits in his penguin mask. His long beak was pointed and sharp like a razor. He was going to end her life.

There was blood. It poured in buckets onto the grey road that separated her childhood home and school; a road she had travelled thousands of times, and one she now avoided since her brother's death there. The brambly hedges and thorny bushes at either side of it poked at her, forcing her to look at what she had done, at what she had caused. She saw the car, a red '96 Ford Orion, and woke up clinging to her drenched blanket. *Is it normal to grieve after all these years?* she cried inside, wiping tears. *Why couldn't I just wake up?*

Subconscious minds were not to be treated as dumping grounds, she understood. Without mature patrolling, they turned into frenzied dreamweavers, mercilessly juxtaposing random terrifying situations with the familiar content of traumatic memories. She knew that too, and could have done more to prevent the nightmares recurring, she thought, annoyed at her self-negligence.

There were plenty of signs, lead-ups to this grand finale. Her recent dreams had been urging her to pay herself attention, to end her emotional denial. They had turned her once sunny slumber movies a shade darker, warning her that threatening clouds weren't just threatening; that a hard rain was about to fall.

God damn you, mind, she spitted out inside.

2.

Nuala bent over her begonias, green watering can in hand, and reached for the cluster of geraniums at the foot of her red gate, close to the Busy Lizzies. She loved that name, *Busy Lizzie*, and smiled to her dead son Stephen as she imagined Lizzie's human version. He invented the game; a fantasy that required the player to invent their own "man plants." The human/plant being wasn't literally a 'half-in-half' creature, Stephen had explained to his mother in his own words, desperate to make himself clear. They spent the day as plants, the night as humans, never sharing the *same* form.

In the evening, after sunset, when the human versions wandered the earth, he would look out the kitchen window and shout, shake, scream in excitement.

"MAM! There's Rose! She's in a pink dress and LOOK she's got red lipstick on! She's walking across the lawn NOW!"

Nuala had always enjoyed his boundless imagination, even if she some-times wondered if she was encouraging mental dysfunction. But he had only ever used it to distract himself from the slow pace of childhood life in a sleepy town, she consoled herself.

Busy Lizzie, Nuala imagined, was sociable, colourful like a rainbow and well travelled. She had to be. If plant Lizzie could reach across the garden faster and wider than weeds, then human Lizzie would surely want to spread herself around the world. Lizzie was a travelling gypsy. She was common, colourful and loved to keep on the move. Yes, that was her.

Nuala's flight of fancy dropped from the sky in an explosion of grief. She had made the mistake of allowing it to surface; the suffocating weight of the pain that was stronger than she was. She would never stop missing Stephen, never stop longing for him. But there was no need to keep grief, she reminded herself, almost convinced. He was with her now; in the breeze on her face, in the flowers that made her smile. He was everywhere.

"Let" she breathed in, her heart quivering under the strain of what she was about to ask of it, "Go. Let. Go."

In a last heave of will, she gathered the strength to say it and believe it.

"Stephen is safe where he is."

3.

Lillian reached inside her kitchen cupboard and took out the Sainsbury's maple syrup. Nothing cut through a thick mental haze like syrup, she thought, drizzling it in swirls over her pancakes. At a billion calories, it was a bold choice, but this morning wasn't like any other morning. Only sweetness could kick-start this miserable day, she decided early on.

She sat at the table and thought about crying. It would be easy to just cry it out; to surrender to the quivering lump in her throat that wanted out.

But what if I can't stop? she thought, afraid of her own weakness. She had spent enough hours reading self-development books to know that happiness was a responsibility, not a given.

I just need to use my best behavioural tools to feel better, is all.

She was serious about happiness and wasn't going to give in to the night-mares attempting to take her over.

Her time alone was spent with the most challenging texts on the human condition: Goldman, M. Scott Peck—the good ones. She knew her Plato, about his cave allegory, about how humans are blinder than they know. She especially knew that no good could come out of languishing down the phantom corridors of her pained past. There were enough depressives in the world engaging with their 'lower emotions.' She had let him go a long time ago; it was time for her mind, all parts of it, to do the same. It was time for work.

She plopped her saucer into the sink, skipped to the hall, picked her beige jacket from the over-tasked coat stand and let the door slam behind her.

She thrived on the bustle of London in the morning. Her home in the South East of Ireland was buried inside the valley of an insular community; a place where Catholic Novenas were the highlight of the year. But London, her sweet adopted city, pulsated with life.

Her tube line to work had been stitched in silver thread into its own neural pathway, freeing her of the cumbersome task of conscious navigation. It was a part of her mind that liked to work without supervision; a guardian whose job it was to guide her safely around the intestines of her city, through all its bends, turns, climbs and descents, without her full attention.

Her morning headscape was the perfect breeding ground for thoughts that preferred to project neuroticism outward onto others. Lillian had no waking awareness that she hosted such a quirk, and as she walked a steady gait she tutted righteously at the sight of mad hatters watching clocks who were, she assessed, so obsessed with reaching their next destination they couldn't be present in the moment.

She played with her long pendant chain as she stood on the platform and waited for the tube, alternating the activity with a split-end inspection of her blonde curls. After a few seconds the train whistled as it rushed out from the tunnel, its breeze ruffling people's newspapers and the raggedy edges of torn advertising posters. She expertly made her way to the top of the queue and waited for the doors to part. Averting the eyes of her competitors, she claimed a seat and scanned the carriage for interesting-looking people.

That skinny woman's marriage is in trouble. She's a newlywed. The ring on her finger is worth more than Guatemala. Her husband is rich and good for her security. But now she feels like she sold out. She's in doubt, always—about everything. She's asking herself who she is, what she wants, where she's going. It all happened so fast.

She wrapped it up with a prognosis: self-honesty and divorce, and moved on to her next case.

That suited banker man type is incubating. Western material culture has its claw around his ego. He's driven by boundless desire. Eventually he'll find that it's all empty and sell his condo to live in India.

No time for more, she thought, reaching her eyes over the crowd from her tiptoes. Packed carriages made it difficult to confirm her stop, but as the exit doors swished open, clearing a space, she caught a glimpse of the familiar totems that told her she had arrived. She hopped onto the platform, took two steps at a time up the escalators and ran for exit 5, towards Whitehall; to her office at London's top charity.

She beeped her staff pass through security labyrinths to the lift. The glass elevator doors parted at level four, on Marianne: head of PR. The Press Queen, an accolade Marianne had awarded herself, was a tough competitor. Singlehandedly, she raised the profile of Care about Children UK from barely-there NGO to globally recognised super charity. Lillian figured she spent her spare time bending metal into poodle shapes.

Some people just clash, Lilian would remind herself when she felt bad about disliking her.

Lillian had done some psychometric tests online and discovered, to no surprise, that achievement was the focal point of her life. A friendly relation-ship with another success orientated personality was an unrealistic ambition. It didn't help that Marianne had recently publically humiliated Lillian at a staff meeting. The Press Queen had stood tall on her Laboutin feet, in view of everyone, and praised Lillian for having the humility to grovel to the Polish Ambassador.

A month before, Lillian had made a 'holy show' of herself, by her own ad-mission and had already apologised for it. The incident that led to the much-hyped 'I'm sorry' was fairly harmless, in Lillian's view, and didn't deserve the level of attention it had attracted. She had been standing in the conference room her charity had rented for a seminar. She was waiting to greet guests, chief of which was the Polish ambassador. The water bottles were laid out, the name signs laminated, clearly visible and spelled correctly. She was seeing to final touches, laying a paper and pen on everyone's seat, when an impatient man walked in and interrupted her, demanding to know where the toilets were, to which she replied, in a throaty tone:

"This is a *private* room."

When his blank expression demanded more attention, she delivered a second blow with bullet spray speed: "Ask-someone-who *knows*-where-the-public-toilets-are-what-am-I-a-tour-guide?"

When he opened his mouth to protest, she told him to get lost.

She couldn't have predicted the consequences, or that the man was the Polish Ambassador.

I mean, who lets an ambassador wander alone around a hotel looking for toilets?

It was all she could say in defence. It had been an uncharacteristic assault, and one that left her shamed. It was an uncomfortable journey to the part of the emotional spectrum she associated with Neanderthals and not with 'emotionally intelligent' people like herself. She blamed it on peaking period hormones. They, the evil molecules of darkness, turned her mind into a cesspit of boiling, bubbling, molten lava. The molecules needed, they required, at least one eruption a day for relief. "Every pressure system needs a relief valve," Lillian later told her friends, attempting another justification for her bad behaviour.

After her respectful apology that day to the ambassador, which she offered in humility, she returned to the office, where her rage resurfaced. She let the second outburst out by the water cooler, safe, she unwittingly assumed, in the company of the temper-chilling machine.

"As if," she said to her colleagues, "a man could understand a hormonally induced explosion. Well…"

As Lillian sniggered at her unintended joke, Marianne saw her opportunity.

'That's right, Lillian, blame your outbursts on *hormones*. It had nothing to do with your…immaturity?'

She delivered the sting with typical composure and walked breezily on, leaving Lillian seething.

Since that day, she had been making an impressive effort to seem cool in front of Marianne. Today, first day of a long working week, she stepped out of the elevator, Audrey Hepburn-style.

"Good morning, Marianne."

Marianne took a dramatic step backwards and scanned Lillian's face.

"Hungover?"

Lillian, unmoved, responded flatly.

"No. You bring out that look in me. I think it's just…disgust."

Marianne screeched into laughter as Lillian passed her on her way to her desk.

The office at Care about Children was 'cheery,' according to one researcher with the *joie de vivre* of a kid's TV presenter. Optimism and gusto were encouraged over the 'outrage' and 'anger' that fuelled all other humanitarian organisations. The about us section of the website used the words 'innovative' and 'groundbreaking' every other sentence, as did its pamphlets, advertising campaigns and any other medium its press machine used for self-expression. The least management could do to support such claims was decorate it boldly. It was open plan and open hearted, as the geeky designer had said, and splashed artfully in mosaic maps of successful expatriate missions. At the bottom of the office, above the boss' headquarters, a flat screen TV played the Organisation's latest fundraising campaign on a loop.

"Hiiiiiiiii, Scott" Lillian cooed, approaching his desk.

If something went wrong, Scott fixed it, but otherwise he got paid for facebooking. Dressed in a trademark funny t-shirt *'Make awkward sexual advances, not war',* horn-framed spectacles and a high-trend hair cut, he looked the chic London metrosexual.

"Still single?"

Since women were his life's chief focus, it was a standard Monday morning question.

"Actually, Sarah's waitress friend got a bit cheeky with me on Friday night...but she just wanted a free drink. I tell you, you can take the girl out of Liverpool but you can't take the..."

"Don't finish that sentence..." Sarah whispered, pointing her head towards agro-head Rosie-who'd-do-anything-for-a-fight in the corner, from Liverpool.

...And anyway, she's not a waitress—she's a model. And she wouldn't kiss you for a contract with Rodarte. Let's face facts here."

"She's a bum is what she is."

Sarah was the only other girl in the office from Ireland.

Lillian walked on, shouting her response to her over her shoulder.

"Keep him away from your girlfriends. He's a perv."

She stopped to fill her dented water bottle at the cooler, where this morning there were just two gossipers: pregnant Lisa from admin and Trish from marketing. They stopped talking abruptly as Lillian positioned the neck of her bottle under the flow of extra cold water.

" 'Ello Lillian.'

"Hi, Trish."

"Did you hear about Tina?"

"No," Lillian replied bluntly, expressing her disinterest. She removed the bottle before it was tip-top full and rushed to her desk, where a pink post it on her screen made her hairs stand.

'Meeting at 11am sharp in the blue room, Richard.'

Fucking great.

4.

He, the boss, the number one man, paced the floor of his spacious office in lanky strides, assuring himself he was up to the challenge ahead. There were going to be changes, progress even, he thought to himself, white knuckled. It excited and unnerved him. Innovation was something he was used to dreaming about, not achieving. He'd spent months working up to this.

His experience in the predictable environment of the civil service had accustomed him to gross hype about *progress*: a word politicians used for keeping things the same. His whole department was an 'old dog,' he would whine. And it simply 'killed' him to embroil himself in such 'inconsequential professional activity.' There was a world out there to change and he was going to do it.

Incurable idealism was his earliest affliction, his greatest fuel. It was only a matter a time before the Phoenix rose from the ashes, he would warn his civil service colleagues, who would burst into laughter at him. As if he would leave the security of a government job for a flimsy dream, they would tease—which made it all the sweeter when he did.

His career change started with a blown gasket; a stretched-to-the limit feeling that he could no longer put up with. He was done talking himself round with a rationale that championed mortgage repayments over authentic ambition. So he left. Just like that. It was time, he resolved, to return his allegiance to the free-wheeler in him. It was time to follow his dream. So he gathered his life savings and built Care about Children from nothing.

He took a seat at his desk and indulged heyday memories. He was born with it, this idealism. It was in the remotest and tiniest of his fibres, his every breath. As he looked at the stamped permit on his desk, beaming, he thought back to student Richard.

Can I be that person again? The person who surfed the current of renegade energy beneath the axis of eighties global politics, and loved it?'

Richard's thoughts, like his speeches, were wordy.

He reminded himself that he led the boldest political campaigns the university had ever staged. He stood up to Thatcher's iron-fisted conservative economics. He understood Live Aid and what it all stood for. He exposed corporate America for weaselling its way into developing countries. He even poured red paint over himself—to show them he knew what they were doing, putting blood on the hands of the people. But then he got his girlfriend pregnant and joined the Civil Service. He sold out.

"Hi Richard, I've been waiting for you. It's ten past eleven...you're late?"

Her presence startled him.

"Sorry, Lillian. Pardon me. I've been doing some thinking."

Lillian felt a movement in her gut.

"Oh."

Richard never understood her self-deprecation. At six foot, with a figure that made him think uncomfortable thoughts, and sweet blue eyes, she was stunning. Added to her physical attributes was a sharp intelligence and foresight that surpassed even his elders. Her professional shyness baffled him. He couldn't help but wonder what life experiences would form such a paradoxical character.

"It's nothing bad, Lillian. In fact, it's quite huge. Good huge. Follow me."

Lillian recognised the tone in Richard's voice. He was being reassuring, which she detested, since she wanted to be a force, not a wilting wall flower. She hated her occasional meekness and longed to shake off the little, insecure girl inside her who still partly believed the jeers that girls from Ballybeg couldn't make it big in London.

They walked to the blue room. He was sure she was the woman for the job.

5.

Nuala walked in circles around her country kitchen. She wasn't letting it happen today; no way. She brought the words of her Reiki therapist to mind. The words were supposed to ease moments like this, so she began to affirm them over and over.

"The divine light of God flows within me, creating a life of total peace in my life every day. The divine light of God flows within me, creating a life of total peace in my life every day."

"Stephen is safe and happy where he is. Stephen is safe and happy where he is."

Tears streamed in puddles over her flushed cheeks. She raised her face to the ceiling in an effort to stop them, and berated herself for her weakness, for her lack of courage, her lack of faith.

What's wrong with you, Nuala? It's been almost twenty years. Move on.

She glanced at the fridge, desperate for a distraction, and read the magnet her sister had brought her back from Greece: No man is free who is not master of himself—Epictitus.

She smashed a plate full of last night's leftovers onto the floor in a rage, and shrieked as she choked back more tears.

Pat listened from the hall, fighting the urge to comfort her. What was there left to say? How could he make it better? Today, to the day, it was nineteen years since they lost their son. He stood with his ears to the door and took on his own demons.

6.

Lillian was the fiercest and most formidable person Phil knew. From the first moment he saw her, sitting outside a Camden pub, screeching crying and covered in mascara, he was captivated. *The bastards!* She had screamed to the heavens, *The fucking bastards stole my bag. Again. I HATE this shit hole of a city! Customer fucking service shit hole of the planet.*

You don't mean that, he replied, helping her off the slimy curb she was sitting on.

I do, she sobbed back.

He bought her coffee in an all night café on Tottenham Court Road. He remembered looking at her across the table, listening as she hissed in her Irish lilt at the 'loose morals of the city's vagabonds.' He knew nobody who used the term 'loose morals' or the pejorative 'vagabond,' when drunk, especially an Irish girl. She worked for a charity and wanted to make children 'happy.' He remembered thinking it a beautiful choice of word. She hadn't used 'safe' or 'protected' or any other unambitious word other charity workers he had met used; not this girl Lillian. Lillian wanted children to be 'happy'.

Her temper was one the harshest he had encountered but, intriguingly, love and courage seemed to burst through it in regular intervals, like erupting geysers. It made no sense. She made no sense. It was love at first sight.

Phil never felt his personality matched hers and consoled himself with the "opposites attract" dictum. His family were upper class and reputed, hers were farmers. She spoke to her family in colourful language, he called his uncles Sir. No one spoke outside of convention at his dinner table; at hers, they would fist fight.

Life, to Phil's family, was about maintaining the heavy burden of a first-class reputation, which weighed on him. His mother, who died when he was in boarding school, had been lighter about life than his father. Lillian could never replace her, but she could keep her spirit alive. His mother would have been proud, Phil thought, that the woman he chose had the courage to be herself.

At 32, he had six years on her, a fact that took effort to ignore. Was it even right, he would ask himself, that a young stunner would be attached to him; a shorter, older guy with a larger than average head? Her choice of him was just another thing about her that made no sense; another thing he would never figure out. He would spend his life trying, especially now their 'teething years', as Lillian had eloquently termed them, were over.

He was done with their two-day break-ups, of her tantrums. Lillian had taken his threats to leave seriously and chilled out. He smiled as he turned the key in his office door. As if he would ever have left her, he thought. If she had called his bluff, even just once, he would have begged like a baby for her. But she didn't.

He was first into Clarkson's of London, where leather-bound statutes and precedents stood meticulously in place, row after row, inside glass-cased mahogany book shelves.

His phone vibrated in his pocket. A text from Guy:

"Phil, ya bell end! What's happening this arvo?"

Guy and Phil were recent friends who had met at Phil's engagement party; a night so humiliatingly disastrous it had made Phil consider therapy. Guy had come along with Phil's then fiancé's friend.

Tanya, Phil's girl 'whose shit didn't stink', according to Guy, was a 'masochistic, Nazi-loving, power-tripping see-you-next-Tuesday.' An engagement party wasn't the time or place to dump a fiancé unless you were, as Guy put it, Hitler. She, princess-butter-wouldn't-melt, made it known that she didn't want to be married by flipping out in reaction to Phil's suggestion she be nicer to the waiter while fifty close friends and relatives looked on open-mouthed.

Afterwards, while piecing together the smithereens of his ego, Phil accepted her behaviour had been nothing more than an indirect rejection of his proposal, so he ended the relationship there and then. She had thanked him and left, making Phil feel like the only person in the room who didn't know how much she didn't ever love him. Guy's support that night and afterwards sealed a long friendship, like brothers meeting on a battlefield.

"Heartless bitch," Guy repeated over and over again at the bar after she and all the other guests had left, pouring shot after shot of tequila for Phil. He swapped around other insults, like "she's got a fishing rod for a nose," with "no, a hook. It's more like a hook. And her snots are nuclear."

Phil had been surprised that he was able to hear a stranger tear apart the woman he had intended to spend the rest of his life with. He was even more surprised when Guy urged him to comfort a tall blonde distressed girl sitting on a curb on their way home, and that he listened.

"Go for it, he nudged Phil, "she's beautiful and *vulnerable*. Dead cert."

And that was how Phil met Lillian. It amused him that Lillian never really liked Guy. Her instincts were always spot on, he thought.

"Listen, it'll be evening before I finish, which I think is the...norm? For working people at least. *You* might be free for a grog fest on a Monday, mate, but I'm not."

"Don't be such a stick in the mud. Break loose and come for beeas."

"Guy, we don't all work for our uncle. And it's Monday."

"Exactly, mate. Hair of the dog. Come on."

Submission, Phil realised, was the easiest option.

"Meet you at six. Old Street Station."

Phil's boss Ray entered the office as he dropped the phone.

"Philip, did you take a look at the Gibson case?"

'Yes."

"I want you to *really* look at that case. There's no precedent, no common law ruling—there's nothing to base it on, besides a very ambiguous European Convention. We're going to need serious focus on this one. I mean, does our chap have a strong case? Give me answers. Blow me away.'

He gathered memos from Debbie the stunning secretary's desk.

"Coffee please, Debbie," he shouted from his office.

"His knickers are on fire today, Philly"

Debbie's chestnut hair was as soft as her cockney-accented voice. She had just accepted an offer from Ray to pay her way through evening college.

"He wants our balls on this one, Debs. You might get at chance at some real experience. Well, research anyway...which *is* great experience."

"Yes, maybe."

Phil noticed her directing her eyes shyly back to her computer screen. He knew she was wandering if she had what it took.

"No, not maybe—definitely."

7.

Lillian sat startled at her desk.

Everything she ever wanted was coming at the worst possible time in the worst possible combination. Alanis Morissette's song about the black flies in chardonnay played in her head.

And isn't it ironic, don't ya think? A little toooooo ironic.

Life, now, was as catastrophically ironic as the man afraid to fly; the man who packed his suitcase and kissed his kids, and ass, goodbye.

How am I supposed to feel? she asked herself, head in hands.

Anger stepped up to the plate with an offering, a righteous penny's worth: *Happy, you idiot, you're supposed to feel happy.*

Emotion sucked her thoughts into a giant twister, using neuroticism as fuel to dance its righteous dance. It spun in circles; flirted with the wattled towers of her sanity; took her over.

A little toooooo ironic, it blew, oblivious to her anguish.

She raised her sunken head out of her hands and straightened her spine. She had work to get on with. She'd deal with the monkeys in her head later.

8.

The Press Queen and her puppy dog Victoria sat in the staff kitchen over hot cups of peppermint tea. Victoria loved to emulate Marianne's behaviour, down to dietary choices. She was a first class sycophant, a keen player in the vanity fair that characterised Marianne's world. She knew that to get ahead she had to play to her boss's arrogance. Her unwavering collusion supported some of Marianne's foolish illusions about her own greatness, but Victoria wasn't going to put her own progression at risk by undoing Marianne's self inflated ideas about herself. She was using her to get ahead. It wasn't like Marianne wouldn't do the same thing. Victoria was determined to become a high flying member of London's professional glitterati, just like her boss.

"There's something going on this morning. I sense it. Did you see her after she walked out of his office?"

Marianne loved to gossip, to speculate. She had a passion for interpreting body language. Her totally subjective opinions, however, meant she was regularly wide of the mark.

"Really?" Victoria smiled, fuelling Marianne's rant.

"Do you think it might be serious?"

"I don't know, but I will know."

"Scott, three o'clock."

Sarah threw her eyes right.

"What's happening then?"

"You fool. I mean look to your *right*. Lillian. Look at that face. Something's happened. I'm going to ask her to lunch; cheer her up. D'ya fancy it?"

"God no. I'm not listening to boyfriend talk or period talk or whatever gets you ladies into strops like that."

"It's not all hormone related, you misogynist"

"Don't insult the shit out of me whatever you do."

"Whatever."

"Standard Sarah response," Scott huffed, "no meat to it."

Lillian filled her water bottle. She knew they were talking about her and tried to make eye contact with Scott, whose whip-lash inducing twist on his swivel chair alerted her.

Can't they just mind their own business?

Sarah read the wordless exchange and approached Lillian tentatively, understanding she wasn't comfortable with vulnerability.

"Fancy a nice long lunch in St James' park? We could get fruit in Tesco's and plop ourselves under a tree? "

"Love to."

"It's a date!"

Lillian made her way back to her desk and tried to talk herself round. An old gramophone record of overplayed doubts and fears clashed with the white noise of anxiety. To get through times like these, she would employ The Controller; the dominant voice, the Chief Whip. The Controller was the superhero in her; the part that sheared doubts with a machete.

You have work to do. Get on with it.

There was no arguing with The Controller.

9.

Marianne wrapped her knuckles on Richard's door with one hand, using the other to button up her ruffled Burberry trench coat. The weather didn't require it but she felt it deserved a parade.

"Are you about ready, Richard?"

She peeped her porcelain face around his slightly open door, a beautiful, raised eyebrow animating it.

"I suggest the Lion's head on Parliament Street for lunch. It's a good old fashioned 'ye-olde' British pub. And so snug."

Richard felt she was trying to be 'earthy,' which she knew he liked.

It's all strategy with that girl.

"Sounds good. I'm ready."

They made their way down the main office corridor in brisk, synchronised strides.

Lillian looked up sheepishly at them, wondering how their conversation would go.

That street rat better not try to talk him out of it.

As she listened to the thought she realised that maybe she wanted the job more than she had been letting on.

"So, Richard"

Marianne's tone was serious.

"I'm sensing that something big is happening at Care about Children. Am I right?"

She was always right.

"Yes, you are."

"Go on..."

Marianne's impatience entertained Richard.

"Richard, come on! Seriously."

"OK, alright! I've been in contact with the Vietnamese Committee for foreign NGOs—as you know. We've finally got the permit."

Marianne's mouth hung open.

"Wow!' We *do* have a lot to talk about. This is exciting, Richard. Wow! We've wanted Vietnam for *so* long."

He was pleased with her response. Emotion fuelled passion, and when Marianne was on fire, she was unstoppable.

"I'm glad you think so. It's important that you really believe in this."

"I do! And I'm going to pull out all the stops. First, I'll get in touch with the UN's Committee for NGOs—we'll definitely be getting consultative status on the Economic and Social Council now. And there's every chance we can start getting press coverage in the European media, too."

"It's great to see you this way. I can't say Lillian was as rapturous when she heard...

His tone softened

…but I suppose it's a bigger deal for her."

"Oh, yes? Why?"

"I'm surprised you ask, Marianne."

"Why?"

"She's development officer?"

"Yes?"

"She'll be *leading* the project in Hanoi?"

Marianne looked dumbstruck.

"She'll have to move. She'll be alone for the first month."

"Oh, right…For some reason I presumed you'd hire *new* people with *expatriate* experience. Wouldn't that be wiser, Richard?"

"Lillian has travelled the world—that *is* experience. And she does have experience; she worked for a few months on the Guatemala project. She's good with people, she cares and she's going to make us a lot of contacts over there. I'm confidant about that."

As he opened the door in front of them, Richard coaxed her into agreement with a firm look.

"Yes, I suppose you're right. She's the logical choice."

I0.

It was six o'clock and time to go home. Lillian skimmed over her report brief and read over the same old story.

> 'UNICEF has accused the UK of failing children, rating it last in a league table for child wellbeing across 21 industrialised countries. The Government has responded by saying its policies have improved Child Welfare.'

Of course they have.

The Controller, her internal Chief Whip, urged her to keep cool.

"Uncontrolled emotions cast people out of the excellence zone," it reminded her.

She invited her higher reasoning to trump the influence of her reptilian brain; the part that wanted to strangle slimy politicians.

The way those greaseballs avoid blame would make a bomb-thrower blush.

'She tried hard to fight anger, but too often lost the battle.'

'The UK Child poverty rate has doubled since 1979.'

That's a fact that couldn't be denied, she smiled, tilting it into Italics and underlining it in size 14 font.

Plain. Simple. Obvious.

She looked over the case she had chosen as the report's main focus.

'The Baby X case has once again exposed systemic failings in the UK's child protection services. Baby X had two broken legs when he died. The emotional damage is incalculable. He was known to social services.'

She resisted the urge to curse out loud. It was beyond comprehension and totally unforgiveable, she thought.

They can't possibly defend themselves against the tragic story this child's life turned out to be.

'This latest death came after a major overhaul of services in 2004 following the tragic death of Victoria Climbie. One of the most important recommendations of Lord Laming's report, which came in the aftermath of her brutal death, was the implementation of 'joined-up' thinking between various child protection bodies, as well as the NHS and the police.'

No such new thinking has been achieved, she wrote, clicking send, cc-ing Marianne and Deepa from policy. Done.

She wished everything else in her life could be as simple as a tick on a to-do list. Hanoi. Had she really agreed to move to *Hanoi*? Without even consulting Phil? What was the place even like? Besides some presentations from the research team about it, she knew little. Richard had given her a week to decide. But, to assure him she was a strong minded adult who didn't do vacilation, she looked him straight in the eye and said yes. YES. She thought about it now; about how easy it had been for her to just throw a grenade into her relationship. What a waste of effort fixing things and reading how-to-improve-your-relationship books. What a mess, she thought, ruefully. Was she really that vulgar? That selfish?

She threw her pink cotton bag over her shoulders and switched her computer off. She wished a window's pop up box would invite her mind to do the same.

The flat sound of her tasselled boots echoed through the spiralling fire escape as she fled two steps at a time towards the fresh air outside, where she rummaged for her blackberry.

"Hey, how was your day?"

"Superb. Yours?"

"Not superb."

"Oh. You probably don't want to hear that I'm meeting Guy for drinks, then."

"Can't say I'm delighted, no. But it's fine. I'm fine. Just be home before ten so we can talk. And don't be late, Philip."

"Philip?! What have I done to deserve *Philip*?"

"Nothing, *Phil*! Just don't come in falling around on your arse."

"I'll be sober as a judge, or barrister, if that'll do."

"That wasn't a joke."

"Was so! I have to go now, I see Guy's across the street. See ya!"

Phil had been really happy lately, she acknowledged, feeling guilt rumble her insides. And now she was going to ruin it. Again. How could he understand why she had done it: agreed to go to Hanoi, when she didn't herself? She thought she wanted things to stay as they were; that she was happy. She thought she wanted marriage, responsibility—a mortgage, even. But now, as she made her way to the station, she was beginning to wonder if it was for nothing. Would she really be willing to uproot if she was truly in love?

She walked slowly from the tube to their apartment and pleaded with herself for honesty. Was he the one or did she just want a beach wedding? What was love? How was a person supposed to know if they were in it? It wasn't as tangible as getting into, say, a car, and realising, yes, I'm in a car. If only. But if she was honest about it, and she had already decided to be honest, there *were* tell-tales, like butterflies, sweaty palms, loss of appetite. That's how a person knew. She had never had those symptoms with Phil.

But she had them with Jake.

A golden thought bubble rained down.

She was on the leopard print couches of a theatre-turned-club in Camden with her English cousin, aged 18, awkward and red faced from the heat. He strolled cool as a cucumber into her space and winked. Her legs fainted.

He was a poet, dripping sensitivity and effortless style. Unflappable confidence oozed from his green eyes, impressing the shy, younger Lillian. A single stroke of his gentle hand through her hair made her immobile. She recalled the letters he used to write her, how he would hide them in her bag without her knowing, how she would gush her brains out. She made it her business to spend the rest of her summer holidays in London and begged her parents demented.

The day she caught him kissing another girl on London Bridge was the beginning of a dark time in her adolescent life. Standing rigid across the street, lips quivering, she felt the unbearable pain of her first broken heart tear up her insides. It was total devastation. She would never, ever, she firmly resolved, get carried away by lust or romance again. Jake, the rat bastard, extinguished her faith in perfect love. She returned to Ireland after her summer break and cried for a month.

She laughed hard, thinking back. She had always been so intense.

At thirteen, an older boy she met at a sports event changed her way of thinking. The girl who considered herself a focused and fierce competitor turned flippant overnight. *Who cares?* She had shouted as she danced like Beyonce in front of him on the basketball court dance floor, *We're in Mosney!*

He was from Northern Ireland, like his accent. She would listen to his ascending tones and stare at his sculpted face with the subtlety of a curious three-year-old. They kissed once, very briefly on a beach beside the athlete's village. Neither could look the other in the eye the day after. When the weekend ended, he—she had forgotten his name—plucked up the courage to ask for her number. She remembered the taunts of everyone around, the whistling and jeering- and the heat of her embarrassment as she turned crimson. She felt like a movie star.

Phil. Well. . .for one thing, his mechanical thinking balanced her flightiness. Without her, he was wooden; without him, she was in space. It was a truly symbiotic relationship, like the fish that swim with sharks.

But was she madly in love with him?

The question played on a loop.

What did she even want out of life?

She turned the key in the door and plonked onto her sofa.

Who was she?

Another golden thought bubble.

This time, it was about the older men in her life; her earliest role models.

At the age of six she developed the habit of knocking on her lonely neighbours' doors asking them to make her tea—so she could keep them company. John Harney, the bachelor, had always rejected her.

"Why doesn't John like me?" she had asked her mother.

"Because John doesn't like *anyone.*"

Young Lillian was baffled.

"But will he like me if I'm nice?"

She never could accept rejection and did everything to avoid feeling it. After the accident, when her brother died, her father withdrew his affection. Her aversion to men deepened.

Her thought bubble turned to bronze.

After the crash the most important role model in her life retired from his role as her father. *I quit* he might as well have said to her face. *I quit as your father because I don't love you anymore.*

And John, what an asshole, she hissed.

John was cruelly unresponsive to her, a young idealistic little human who hadn't been trampled on by life. He probably resented her for it. She was glad, looking back, that she had given up on his sorry ass. All she wanted was to shake him out of the pathetic condition that seemed to plague the men in her life—idiocy.

Despite them, she was confident about her ability to do good. And Phil would just have to realise that protecting children from cruel male adults was her life's purpose; and that she needed to go to Hanoi.

She crafted her plan. She would point out that it wasn't her decision; that she hadn't put herself forward for the job, which wasn't a lie *per se*. Then she would tell him that it would only be for three months—to begin with—and he could come out to see her for a couple of weeks for a holiday.

Her phone vibrated against the granite counter.

'MAM CALLING'

"Hiya"

"Lillian! I was calling to see if you were dead or alive."

"Well, since I answered..."

'How's work?'

"It's good, mam. Nothing new."

Because her mother inspired the stereotype of the nosy Irish country woman, Lillian held back on her news. Better than dealing with congratulatory facebook postings before she told her boyfriend, she thought.

"And Philip, how is he doing?"

"He's great"

"Is he there with you now?"

"Nah, he's gone to meet a friend for drinks"

She kicked herself for letting it out.

"Of a Monday! Isn't it well for him? And you're always saying how he has such a heavy caseload"

"Mam, he's perfectly entitled to go out and meet his friends. He was in all weekend buried in his books."

Why am I telling her that? Do I really still need my mother's approval?

"He'd do better to go out at the weekends and do his bit of study during the week, wouldn't he? Like everyone else?"

She increased in pitch when dishing unwelcome advice. Lillian stayed quiet, uhm-hmm-ing her way through the conversation.

"Mam, I really have to go. I'm peeling veg here"

"You'd want to go down to the butcher and get some meat for yourself. I don't understand this vegetarian malarkey. You need Iron, Lillian."

"I get plenty. And do you cow chewers not understand that iron is available in a WIDE variety of vegetables and grains?! Mam, you don't need to SLAUGHTER for iron. Killing is actually quite an extreme measure, when you think about it. "

She felt guilty for being obnoxious, but was tired of her mother's negation of vegetarianism as a sensible lifestyle choice. If she thought that being vegetarian was a precursor to losing bone density and vitality, it was Lillian's job to explain to her it wasn't. It was always better to keep the debate nutrition related, since Lillian didn't want to explain the real reason she was vegetarian was because she genuinely believed it cruel to kill animals for food when it clearly wasn't necessary.

"Hmmm, alright love. I'll let you go. Don't leave it so long until the next time. Love you."

"Love you too. Say hello to dad for me."

Lillian's father never came to the phone. Sending vicarious greetings to him was more of an involuntary reflex, a nicety she still felt obliged to fulfil. When he answered the phone, she'd get a quick hello. Then, he would give his signature line:

"I'll get your mother"

As a child with a cut knee:

"I'll get your mother"

As a terrified teenager sobbing over a broken heart:

"I'll get your mother"

Calling home with news of 'outstanding' exam results:

"I'll get your mother"

She could imagine how he wouldn't respond when her mother passed on her best wishes.

She blamed his stoicism for most of her own emotional shortcomings. Her hypersensitivity to criticism and over-achieving personality were directly caused by his glacial presence. Nothing she ever accomplished endeared him to her.

It was his fault that her personal development was stunted; that she has a desperate longing in her for emotional restitution.

She slammed the phone down onto the counter.

Screw him.

II.

"Mate, stay for one more. Check out the pins on boobs in the corner."

"I'm happy with what I've got, mate."

"C'mon, you can look if you promise not to taste. No harm in that, no harm at all."

"I'm off. We're having 'a talk' tonight."

"You're in for it, definitely."

"In for a shag."

Phil laughed as he swigged his dry martini back.

"Right. I can actually see your camel toe already—gonna make having sex with a chick pretty hard, that creeping condition of yours."

"You're a sick boy."

"Just be sure not to hit your vagina on the way out."

Phil stuck him a lewd gesture, pulled the brass poll of the door and headed for Liverpool Street Station confident, despite Guy, that a sexy night in was ahead of him. He noticed bouquets of daises walking past Marks and Spencers.

Petals would be a nice touch.

"Oh, hi. Oh, and you brought flowers. That's sweet."

Her unconvincing tone hit him like a punch in the gut.

"Lillian, what is it? You're killing me. First you call me 'Philip' then you barely bat an eyelid at the flowers. What's going on?"

She seemed absent, guarded.

She's cheated on me.

He waited for her confirmation.

Her eyes started to water.

Jesus Christ, I'm right!

His heart kicked.

"Phil, Richard...

She looked to the floor, as though she were to talking to it.

...He wants me to..."

"To what, Lillian?"

"To lead a new project in Hanoi. I have to relocate to Vietnam for three months."

Ha-noi. Vi-et-nam. The words punched him in the brain.

She paused and scanned his face.

He let out the only words he could.

"I...thought we were finished."

She laughed nervously and reached for him.

"We can get through this, Phil. I can't say I would have…chosen this for us…especially not now, but I…I won't let anything come between us. We've come too far."

"When do you leave?"

"Three weeks."

"Oh."

"I know."

"Oh, right."

"Phil, are you OK? You seem a bit…spaced out."

"I've just been hit with a bomb, Lillian. Jesus Christ, give me a second here."

'It'll take time. I'm not saying it won't take time."

"Glad to hear it," Phil said dryly as he removed the cap from a bottle of beer.

"How about we go to Frank's for a nice Italian?"

"Fine."

Lillian dived into a monologue about illegal child adoption as she grabbed her coat. Her eyes widened as she spoke. There was nothing to do, Phil realised, but listen and feign interest.

12.

It was 7am and Marianne was busy. She spent the night chewing on practical logistics; the software needed for new advertisements, contacts to call on, the marketing angle. Taking care of basics first instead of rushing into the bigger picture was a recipe for success. She had a long established *modus operandi*: build a strong foundation and move on to brick work. It was the right way. The only way.

She would need to open the communication channels with the mainstream media, policy think tanks, international NGOs. Ideas streamed in whirlpools. She ate lists, facts, statistics, knowledge.

Who'll write the mission statement for our fundraising campaign? Deepa in policy. . . .
How are we going to market this? And what will we call the project? Nothing too wordy. . .
Vietnam Vic. . .tims? Rubbish. What about a strong visual on the fundraiser stationary? Victoria.

"Victoria! Get in here."

Victoria was beside her in a second.

"I need you to take notes. Just listen to me and write. You'll need your shorthand. Go and get a notepad and give it a title. You're only to use the notebook for the Hanoi project. Is that clear? There's no room for confusion on this one, Victoria!

"The Hanoi project?"

Victoria's bemused expression begged for an explanation.

"I don't have time. You'll eventually get it. Now get that notebook."

She rushed back as though she were taking notes for the Prime Minister.

"OK, first thing's first. People I need to contact: The UN Committee for NGOs, the Department of Foreign Affairs, the British embassy in Hanoi, Hanoi-based children's charities, the Vietnamese Minister for Children...

...Deadline for making contact is 2pm on Friday. Highlight that please, Victoria. We have to work to deadlines."

She paced the floor, one hand on her high-waisted fendi skirt, the other rubbing her upper lip.

"Grant applications next, then written communication to the department of foreign affairs. And we're going to need to think about marketing this. We need input. I need to call a meeting. Tomorrow should be good. Send an email to everyone. I need everyone in on this. Tell Richard he can give the news at the beginning of the meeting. I'll follow with a presentation. Do that, then come in here and I'll tell you what I want on my power point. The meeting will be first thing. Go."

Victoria looked panicked.

"But you haven't told me about the project. What should I put in the email?"

Her hapless look annoyed Marianne.

"Just call a meeting and say it's important—that it relates to a new project. Use your initiative, Victoria. Now go. I want it done yesterday."

13.

"OK, it's time to let me in on it. What's going on? Why are we all being herded into a meeting first thing tomorrow? Am I screwed?"

Scott was nervous. Yesterday had been weird. First Lillian trudged out of Richard's office with a face like a slapped arse; then Richard and Marianne had a hush-hush lunch liaison. Now management was calling everyone together.

Oh God, what if they're making cutbacks?

He'd be the first to go. What if he was forced back to the North? There was no way he could afford to stay in London without his job. He could see himself eating pasties on his mother's velvet couch.

No way.

"I can actually see your mind racing off like a steam train. Listen, I'm not supposed to tell you this, but there's going to be a new project. It'll be based in Hanoi. Lillian's going to have to move. She was sad yesterday because she has to leave her lover man."

"Nice one. *Re-lief.*"

"Am...*insensitive!*"

"I mean the news about the project. Lillian will be sweet—she's just being self involved. There's no need for her to be miserable. What's her misery? Taking a step up the career ladder? Yes, my heart bleeds..."

Sarah giggled, though she felt she shouldn't, and threw a paper ball at his head.

"You're some prick, Scotty."

"You'd know."

"What's going on here?"

Lillian's teleported presence took them by surprise.

"Oh...nothing."

Lillian twitched her nose.

"Then why do I smell lies?"

"Scott was just making shit-smelling banter."

Don't they ever mix it up? Lillian thought.

"Do you guys wanna have lunch outside today? It's another cracker out there."

"I'm up for it."

Scott had strategically placed his measuring ruler upright from his groin.

What a child.

"That's quite a convincing penis. Well done, Scotty," Lillian said.

She might as well speak to him like one, she thought.

"Don't leave me alone with *that*."

Sarah's tone was as flat as her new mood.

"See you guys at one."

Lillian left.

"Did you get a whiff of that sex panther perfume?"

Sarah turned from Scott, burying herself into paperwork to avoid him.

"I was only saying."

"I'm ignoring you."

"Right. No more rude-boy antics out of me. You're a lady, Sarah. You don't deserve to be subjected to my heinous musings. I'm a monster."

He strained his neck over the low parting separating their desks, close enough to see her eyes widen in a smile.

"AHA!"

"Scott, get some work done. You're annoying me."

14.

The office mood had shifted. As he looked through the glass door of his office, Richard felt excitement. *Imagine,* he thought to himself, *that it's possible to feel excited about work.* He grinned at Victoria's red cheeks as she typed furiously. He noticed how Lillian was dressed more professionally than usual; how Marianne's office door was closed, which meant she was even more focused than usual. *Wonderful.*

It was time to start thinking about finer details. He thought about his staff; about who he could get on board, who would relocate to Hanoi.

The Irish girl Sarah was good at her job, he thought, and handed in reports on time. *And* she was a good number cruncher, one of the few he had. She'd be good with logistics. Her boyish personality made her tough. He was looking for tough. *Maybe.*

He thought about phoning his employment agency; getting them to design job profiles for the Hanoi project. He picked up the phone receiver.

"Marianne, I need you in my office."

"Can't it wait Richard? I'm really quite busy."

"Now, Marianne."

He rarely used his authority so blatantly. She almost liked it.

"Right, if you insist."

She walked brazenly into his office, arms folded as she stood over his desk.

"What is it, Richard?'"

"I need you to help me thrash out some ideas. I need to think about new staff, organisational matters, legal issues, all that jazz."

"With all do respect, Richard, I'm a press officer—not a HR consultant. Or a lawyer. I'm paid to do *one* job."

The nerve of her.

It pained him to admit she was right.

"I'm just a bit swamped right now. And we're not a corporate company, Marianne. We're an organisation working to improve lives. We care about people. We're looser with our job specs here."

"You didn't hire me because of my big heart. I never pretended to be Mother Theresa. You know, Richard, feeling concern isn't enough to run a humanitarian organisation. You need people who are smart about doing good, too—not just people going around with their hearts on sleeves."

"You've made your point, Marianne. I'll speak to you later about this week's meeting."

What a cow.

"Great. I was thinking 10am would be good."

"And I was thinking that you don't get to decide. I'll call you when I've decided."

If she was going to be anal about job roles, he was too.

"Fine."

Perfect submission. He was the only boss.

She closed the door. He gathered his thoughts. He needed a partner, an assistant. It wouldn't be Marianne, he now knew. Lillian sprang to mind. She was young at 26, but was clever and committed.

He walked over to her desk, resting half his weight on the edge of her desk.

"Well, how did last night go with the boyfriend? You seem a bit happier today."

His encroachment on her personal life made her uncomfortable.

"Am...good actually. I have his full support, which is a load off."

Feeling conscious about the personal direction the conversation was taking, she changed its course.

"I've been looking up corruption in Vietnam. There's not a lot of information. This is really going to require a lot of digging on our part."

"I knew I made the right choice with you. Look at you, researching already."

"Thank you. I've done loads."

"Actually, I have a list of they key issues we're going to be working on— there's no point in spending too much time researching anything else. I should have given it to you before. We need to stick to those operational activities, since that's what I've told the Vietnamese Government."

Why is he doing the bloody work alone? Why hasn't he involved me in the application process? Grr, Richard, Grr.

"Listen, I want to talk to you about a job promotion. For when you get back. I want you to take some of my responsibilities. You'll get your own office, too."

He was forgiven.

"Great."

"Let's start today. Take a seat at the meeting table in my office. We're going to be consulting on this project every day until it takes off. It'll be practical for you to move into my office until you leave."

"OK"

"And I need us to begin by thinking about staff. I want you to tell me who you want on the project and why you want them. A list would be great, a report would be better."

Lillian picked up the phone as he closed his office door. Jessie.

"Hey! What's the craic, *Oi-rish?*'

"I'm moving to VIETNAM! I'm-the-lead-on-a-new-project-there-and-Phil-is-OK-with-it-and-Richard-my-boss-likes-me-enough-to-promote-me-and-give-me-a-new-office."

"Hold your horses Twinkle Toes. You're going where?"

"Hanoi!"

"NO! NO *way*. When?"

"In a month."

"Why?"

"Really? You care about why it's a month away?"

"No, you bitch, I mean why are you going to Hanoi? Forget it! YOU'RE so *lucky*. Ahhhhh! And here *I* am putting stamps on envelopes for Peace in Darfur."

"How about a get together on Friday? I'll bring Phil and his rich mates. What d'ya say?"

"Phil's mates? As in that hot Australian guy?"

"As in the one *called* Guy?"

"Uhm hmm."

"Oh. I don't actually know about him. He may have a girlfriend."

"Minor issue."

"And he's a bit of an asshole."

"Slanderous talk."

15.

Deepa Shah was an almost perfect person. She emanated calm, gentle positivity. Her deep brown eyes and sallow complexion cemented her appeal. She was consistently affable and easy-going. Her time away from the office was spent travelling paths that led to the ineffable.

At work, she stayed in her own bubble, protecting herself from the competitive energy that pervaded the rest of the office. Her unique way of behaving drew Marrianne's attention, who would rant about her to anyone who would listen. *She's a Scientologist, and she's here to recruit.* It was a typical knee-jerk judgement that kept Marianne from knowing anything realer than high fashion.

The first thing Deepa saw that afternoon was Marianne's email about an 'urgent' meeting and a request to coin a title for a new project. She wanted it to be 'marketable.' There was an attachment with further details. Unaltered by the panic in the emails, Deepa got along with her regular duties. She liked being away from the circus downstairs. The only people she had to share a space with were introverted researchers. It was nice and quiet, how she liked it.

"Hi, Deepa. Did you get the email about tomorrow?"

"Lillian!" Deepa smiled, turning around to meet her eye.

"There's going to be a new Project?"

"Yeah. But listen, there's something I wanted to talk to you about."

Deepa had a special ability to spark in others the emotions she herself so effortlessly exuded. Like no one else, she was able to entrain novices to her unique place on the emotional spectrum. It drew people to her, especially Lillian, who greatest ambition was self-management.

"I want, I guess I want…some…coaching?"

Lillian fidgeted with her acorn zip.

"I mean, you came back to work two weeks after your father died, having 'accepted it'."

Deepa had accepted her father's death, but its mention still stirred her. Lillian still hadn't got to the point.

"Well, I was just wondering if…well…I wanted to ask you if I could go on a retreat, or something, with you?"

"Of course. I don't have anything planned though. Are you going through something?"

"Kind of, well, sort of. Not really. I'm just, well….. I'll be leaving the country for a few months and my boyfriend won't be coming and I'm taking on lots professionally and I just want to make sure that I don't lose my…centre, you know? Prevention is better than cure as they say."

Deepa knew what Lillian was really saying was that she didn't want to ever have to feel pain again, and could she help her with that. She knew how the girl in front of her avoided tough emotions and why.

"I understand. That's really responsible of you. I'll plan something and get back to you. Sound good?"

"It does."

"So what's this project about then?"

16.

Debbie called in sick with an excuse about her son getting sand in his eye. Ray was storming around his office, lost without her. Phil wondered how he was going to get through the day.

She was going again. Her stint in Guatemala last year was supposed to be the last of it. She was supposed to tell her boss that. And despite her assurances, he wasn't convinced he'd be able to deal with separation again. She had already broken him twice. He was beginning to wonder if he was a fool.

His mobile phone snapped him out of thought.

"Well, Chief!"

"Son, where were you last weekend? You missed a hell of a time. This year's hunt was the best yet."

Chief was a term of endearment Lillian thought unbecoming of Phil's father. She called him Mr Sutcliffe, to annoy him. He invited her to call him by his first name, Dominic, but she snubbed the offer. Too many times he had brushed her up the wrong way with his neo-liberal diatribes, she would angrily explain to Phil. She had also gone into great detail about how she struggled to share a city with him, let alone a room.

Phil didn't have to think long about why he hadn't gone on the hunt. Lillian would have thrown one of her legendary strops at the thought of him 'murdering' animals. He began to wonder why he let her opinions dictate so much of his behaviour.

"Oh you know why, dad. I didn't fancy telling my vegetarian girlfriend that I was going to shoot animals for fun. I'm after the easy life."

"Don't *ever* let a woman stop you doing what you love."

"I do what I want dad. I think I have to agree with her on the hunting thing, though. It's not exactly harmless, is it? Anyway, whoever said hanging a head over a fireplace made you a man was deluded."

"Son when you get the hairs on your chest back we'll talk about this rationally. Anyway, the reason I called: I'll be up the East End on Saturday meeting a few friends. I'll pop in when I'm done. What time suits?"

Dominic had a habit of inviting himself places. Today it was more amusing to Phil than annoying.

"We'll be home, dad. Pop by around noon. It'll be great to see you."

"Right, I shall see you both then. In the meantime, do see a chiropractor about straightening that spine of yours!"

Phil dropped his phone and got back to the case in front of him. An A-list celebrity had hired the firm to take action against a tabloid for splashing a defamatory headline over the front page and juxtaposing it with a grimy picture. It was a typical character assassination. The paper, Phil's client claimed, had hacked into his voicemail and stolen private information.

There was no way it was in the public's interest to know about this actor's sexual trysts, Phil thought. The guy wasn't married, so an *alleged* threesome with prostitutes was definitely of no interest to the public—whether it happened or not. The editor was claiming fair comment, which was a tenuous claim at best. Phil could really shine on this one. He began to resent the distraction Lillian had created. It was going to be a long, frustrating day.

17.

It was four o'clock. Lillian was stressed and, now that she thought about it, two weeks late. *Shit*, she spat, as she realised that *once again* she had saved her work—in a million different locations—to her personal computer. No amount of reminders about using public folders could tame her deviant work practices.

"Scott, come with me—*now*. You're gonna be working for the next few hours."

"I don't know what you're implying; I work harder than anyone else in this office."

"Right, I don't actually have time to argue that one out. Come on, let's go."

He arrived at her desk and offered her a card from his party deck. *Not gonna happen*, she told him, in frosty body language.

"I need you to move all my documents, pictures, files—everything—onto one USB. You're gonna have to trawl through the computer to find everything—desktop, documents, Z drive, videos, etc."

Her voice switched to fast-forward gibberish.

"And-don't-even-get-me-started-on-that-printer. I-better-be-able-to-print-to-the-good-printer."

She paused and aggressively drew his eyes to hers.

"And not, I repeat, *not* to the battered lawn mower thing over there. Alright?

"Lawn mower?"

" I refuse to use it."

"Alright, Princess Lillian. We'll sort everything out."

"Right, I'll be moving my things. I need you to sort out the website, too. I've a few articles I want you to upload. I'll leave the hard copy on your desk."

"Why don't you just send a bare-footed messenger in a skirt of reeds? Wouldn't that be easier?"

"What?"

"Copy and paste and—most especially—*email* it to me."

"You want me to mail it to you?"

"That would be *at least* a hundred times more helpful."

Lillian laughed despite herself and sat down, finally, to skim over Richard's manifesto. She'd need to research UN-backed studies about Vietnam, she thought, even though she doubted the infallibility of the over-hyped organisation. But in the same way she accepted politicians, she went along with it and its overstated authority.

What if I'm pregnant? She paused, afraid.

You're not. Now get on with your work.

'While it is difficult to estimate the exact number of Vietnamese children being trafficked, certain trends can be identified. It is estimated that thousands of Vietnamese women and children are trafficked both within and outside the country's borders every year. Due to the secretive and illicit nature of the business, very little is known about the phenomena.'

Lillian launched into another silent diatribe.

"So what are you going doing about it, UN, besides compiling tepid reports, talking and holding conferences?"

She continued to sanctimoniously thrash the shamed-looking UN chair-man in her head. She was brave now, braver than she had been when she had met him in person.

> *'Government efforts include a national plan of action to make sure that all children are registered. Legal protection of children from trafficking in the area of inter-country adoption has been strengthened with new legislation.'*

"Legislation. Of course—because legislation works a treat in a corrupt society. You should be ashamed of yourself, Chairman."

She sat in front of the report and wondered how many well intentioned Western couples had unwittingly caused nightmares for poor rural families in Vietnam. How many of the adoptions went ahead against the child's parents' will? Funny, she thought, and ironic too, that most of the adopted children were born to tribal families—the ethnic minorities that just happened to be the least respected groups in the country. And the poorest. Hardly coincidence.

What kind of shambolic government is letting this happen?

"Richard, what happened in Vietnam after the war?"

Richard was biting on a Granny Smith, wincing.

"Ahuuuum, pardon me. Just a moment."

He held a single finger in the air, put down the mid-afternoon snack and wiped his face. Lillian smiled at him. He was hardly fearsome, she thought.

His voice cleared to firm.

"It was pretty tragic I can tell you. Bloody awful stuff, actually. Sol-diers—who let's just say weren't bright sparks—were awarded high-ranking government positions in reward for their war efforts. So, essentially, the entire Government was built by charlatans with no real abilities. A total mess, really. Not surprising that corruption is rife. Money buys justice in Vietnam, I'm afraid to say."

"It seems so foolish, so short-sighted. And after all that suffering. It just seems so...*she searched for a word.*..blasphemous—to Ho Chi Minh's...philosophy. I mean, their leader, he was so...intelligent. And they loved him. They call him Uncle Ho, for Christ's sake. I can't understand it."

Richard spelled it out.

"Yes, but he died, didn't he? And left chimps to guard his legacy. It happens in developing countries. It's the norm. The people didn't see through it, or maybe they did, but were too tired to fight."

"Well, ya, I'm sure they were."

"Mmm."

Richard paused and thought better of his overly-simplified and subjective summation.

"Of course we can't say that the Government didn't start out with the best of intentions—that just wouldn't be fair. But the foundations weren't solid. Not at all. So in some ways the war went on—if we can simplify war as a struggle between those who dominate those who don't want to be dominated. Of course it's a subtler battle. Because, let's face it, propaganda is a powerful thing. The Vietnamese people don't know how much they're being oppressed, and if they do, they pretend they don't. It's interesting. Take the time to read about it."

"I will."

PRNTER ERROR

"Damn you, Scott!"

Lillian's usual pressure release valve, a deep breath, failed to cool her temper.

"Hello, Scott speaking."

"Scott, why can't my computer 'communicate' with the *good* printer?"

"Uh, I dunno."

"If you spent less time lurking on facebook—and more time on your *work*—you might actually be in with a chance of keeping your job here."

"What's that supposed to mean? Do you know something I don't?"

"Please just do your job and try to act like you care who you piss off."

"It'll take five minutes, tops. Chill fucking out."

"Just get it done."

Maybe I really am pregnant. Oh God.

Breathe, Lillian. It's OK.

Lillian grabbed her bag and ran to the pharmacy.

18.

"Victoria! Get in here."

Victoria was beginning to resent her boss. She had had enough of the Press Queen.

"In a second."

She sat at her desk in a rare act of defiance. Marianne's receptors warned of insubordinance.

"Not then—*now*. Wrap up whatever it is you're doing and get in here."

Was it even legal to talk to someone like that in the workplace? Victoria thought, thinking it better to just submit. She walked towards Marianne and surrendered her ego.

"I need to work on my French. There are oodles of French NGOs in Hanoi. You know. Because of the colonisation business in the past. Or whatever. I don't really care. *Every* European NGO worth working with is French. It wouldn't hurt to have some French. I want to get friendly with their best PR managers. Very friendly. Get me enrolled on a course. A good one. For advanced speakers. Evenings or weekends. That's all."

She was a real pro, Victoria thought. Learning French was galaxies beyond what was expected of her.

Marianne interrupted with an afterthought.

"And type up my power Point for tomorrow. I have the notes here. I hope you can read my writing because I really don't have the time, or energy, to sit down with you."

She smiled at her junior daring her to deny her request. Victoria smiled back in defiance.

"I need it typed up by 4:30. And Victoria, be creative. I don't want people falling asleep on me. I want background audio, too. And decent pictures."

"Sure thing."

Victoria felt her face crack. She was losing more self-respect by the day. But it was worth it. She was learning from the best. Arrogance of Marianne's proportion was fairly rare, but it was backed up by performance, Victoria reasoned. Sucking up was going to pay off.

19.

The meeting was minutes away. Excitement burst into wild chattering, mad speculation. They were making cutbacks. Who would go first? *Surely, the pregnant girl from team C?* Trish offered, who wasn't a fan of pregnant women applying for jobs. *She got that job knowing fine well she were pregnant. She should have said; that's all I'm sayin'.*

Victoria wheeled crates of bottled water into the meeting room. Marianne traipsed coolly around her in a crisp-white shirt, skyscraper heels and a black pencil skirt. Lillian reeled off affirmation after affirmation at her desk. She was going to shine, she was going to shine.

"Alright folks, into the meeting room please."

Richard was wearing the face of a man who was about to give marching orders, the admin girls warned one another.

"I'm sure you've all been wondering what's been going on this past week. In fact, I know you all have. You're all about as discreet as dynamite."

A nervous collective laugh followed on cue.

"I have great news to share with you this morning."

Sighs and smiles moved in a Mexican wave around the table.

"As you know, the Organisation has been growing year after year, receiving more donations on average that most other NGOs in the city. There are many reasons for this, but mostly it's down to the brilliant efforts you all make to raise the profile of Care about Children."

Marianne threw a glance at Victoria, as though to laugh at the idea that it wasn't all down to her.

"Because of your hard work, we are now able to roll out operations to Vietnam, finally! Our operations in Africa and Central America will not be diminished by this. We will still have exactly the same communication with the staff on the ground there as we do now. But workloads *will* increase until we sort out staffing issues. I know that we can make this transition as seamlessly as possible, and I'm happy to answer all questions after the meeting, but for now, I'll hand you over to Marianne, who's going to tell you a bit about Vietnam."

Marianne clicked her fingers at Victoria, a signal to turn the light off and get the equipment ready.

Her presentation opened to images of distressed Vietnamese war children. Lillian recognised the backing track as Hans Zimmer's. *The girl's a hypnotist,* she thought, more nervous than before about her own presentation.

Images of bombed paddy fields, beleaguered villages and limbless children flashed across the screen with statistics.

The Vietnam War created 300,000 orphans

A short pause followed by the second infobit.

800,000 children lost one or both parents. . .in the South alone

Sad eyes exchanged awkward looks around the table.

More than 1.5 million lost their lives

More music, more awful scenes.

The Americans left in 1978

Images of celebrations and parades.

The war is still not over for the country's poorest children.

Next, a staccato of sobering statistics, wrapped up with:

Illegal adoption, child trafficking and physical abuse are rife. Care about Children needs your help. Please donate today and help us to finally put an end to the war against children in Vietnam.

The Press Queen closed to rapturous applause.

Richard stood and gave her an aggressive hand shake.

"Wonderful, that's really wonderful stuff, Marianne."

She let his praise ring through her ears.

"Thank you. Now—to what I want from *you.*"

The crowd ate like goats in a zoo from the palm of her hand.

She had lit a bonfire. Lillian suddenly felt like a fireman's hose.

"Hi everyone," she whispered.

"What Marianne just showed you will have given you a rough idea of what we'll be dealing with in Vietnam...Mine will be a more dressed down presentation."

She paused to will the vomit to stay put in her gut.

Just ten minutes, Lillian. It'll all be over in ten minutes. Hold it together for ten minutes.

"I'll start by telling you about Agent Orange—which all of you will become familiar with over the coming weeks; the various ethnic minorities in Vietnam and their cultural differences, child trafficking, child prostitution and child abuse."

62

The rude bastards are already talking.

"This is a colour-coded map of North Vietnam. You're all going to become familiar with it. Red symbolises the 'hot zones'—as I have so named them—where crimes against children are most rampant. Orange is one level below that, yellow another and green is for the area of least criminal activity."

She could sense the boredom, taste her digestive bile.

"Vietnam is the most Eastern country on the Indochina peninsula. It juts out to the south of mainland Asia and shares its borders with four countries: China to the North, Cambodia to the South West, Thailand to the West and Laos to the North West. It reminds me a bit of Italy actually, but the Vietnamese say it takes the shape of a carrying pole with baskets on either end. Don't ask."

"Nice fact, Lillian. So much for a dressed-down presentation!"

"Trust you, Scott, to fit in a comment about states of undress."

Loud laughing followed.

What can I say, I'm hilarious!

Lillian was encouraged again.

"ANYWAY, the 'basket' to the North is the Red River Valley, the 'basket' to the South in the Mekong Valley, and the 'pole' that runs through the spine of the country is the long, narrow central region of Annam. So there are three major regions."

More chattering.

Insatiable, mannerless pigs.

She spoke over the noise.

"Vietnam is a communist country with capitalist economics. It's a total contradiction but contradiction seems to be the buzzword for Vietnam. I've spoken with Richard about running classes over the coming weeks. There's a lot to learn and more than I can get into this meeting, so I'll start taking groups later this week...

...And guys, if we get this right from the beginning, we can really turn this project into something huge. Vietnamese law dictates that we have to be working on the ground there for at least two years before we can apply for a permit for a representative office. Let's make sure we get it."

Everyone stood up and clapped. Richard smiled as he hushed them.

"I don't want to keep you here all day, but I want to speak now about how we plan on rolling things out. Lillian is going to be leaving in a few weeks to get a base up and running for us. It's important to give her our total support. She deserves great credit for being brave enough to blaze the trail for the rest of us. So, please, stand up again and give her a round of applause."

She called on the burliest of her stomach muscles to hold in the vomit while smiling at the fuzzy, fuzzy crowd.

"Thank you everyone," she let out, bee-lining for the door.

After ten minutes projectile vomiting, Lillian reached for a paper towel to wipe the toxic residue from the seat of the toilet. She walked to the sink, splashed water on her face and looked into the mirror.

And isn't it ironic...

Just get on with your work as though nothing's changed.

She walked like a robot to her computer.

'Agent Orange is a deadly herbicide that was used in the Vietnam War to defoliate the jungles and so prevent Vietnamese soldiers from taking cover there.'

Clever tactic, she thought, *and so effective.*

Her blood simmered. Humans, she was beginning to understand, were capable of atrocities that would make the most hostile animals of the Serengeti flinch. Bringing another into the world was becoming less and less appealing.

Stick to Agent Orange thoughts.

The controller reeled her in.

'The harm caused by the herbicide was much worse at the end of the war than anybody thought...The deliberate and intentioned spraying of such a lethal biological weapon was in blatant contravention of the 1925 Geneva Protocol banning the use of chemical and biological agents.'

Lillian laughed. *As if a Protocol ever stopped anyone! And as if the UN actually has clout.*

The information heated her to blazing.

'A case was taken against corporations for manufacturing the deadly agent in 2004. The plaintiffs alleged that Monsanto Corporation, Dow Chemicals and eight other companies were responsible.'

Lillian laughed cynically and took off with more angry thoughts.

Oh that's new—Multi-million dollar corporations liaising with powerful governments to profit from war and suffering! When will this record play itself out? God! We're such stupid SHEEPle!'

More facts; this time, no laughing.

'In Vietnam there are 150,000 children whose birth defects can be traced back to their parents' exposure to Agent Orange during the war, or the consumption of dioxin-contaminated food and water since 1975'.

She moved from her computer. She was disillusioned now, with everything.

20.

"It was basically fine, but didn't you find it a bit dry? It could have done with a little more, I don't know, va-va-voom."

Has she really just come to tell me that?

"We hire you to be crafty; we hire Lillian to take care of the work we do on the ground. You know, Marianne? The *actual* work? The reason we exist?"

His tone was intended as a weapon against her thick wall of arrogance.

"We wouldn't exist without donations and *they* come from publicity."

It hadn't managed to penetrate it.

"Just do your work. Let Lillian get on with hers."

"I heard her in the toilet, you know. After the presentation."

Richard looked at her, baffled.

"And the movements of Lillian's excretory system are relevant to my life, why?"

"She was vomiting, Richard. She's obviously quite stressed about it. Don't you think you need someone who can handle pressure for a project this big?"

"Marianne, you're not—as you have already made clear to me—my HR consultant. I make the staffing decisions around here. Now, please, close the door behind you."

VICTORIA!

"Yes?"

Victoria looked up through her Jasper Conran specs.

"We're going to lunch. Somewhere where the carpets don't smell like Saturday night's piss."

Oh no, Victoria thought, *she's in a mood*.

"I'll get my coat."

Victoria sat over a mango salad and willed herself to focus.

"I just think Richard is turning a bit. He's beginning to lose his understanding of how successful NGOs are managed. If he's not careful, he'll lose me. Where would he be then?"

"I know. He should really appreciate you more."

"Exactly. How could he possibly take the advice of that Irish bitch over mine?"

"Bitch is a bit strong, Marianne!"

"Sorry?"

Was *she* challenging her, too?

"Nothing."

"I mean, where does she get her fashion inspiration from—the Romanians? Has she *ever* watched a fashion week or picked up a glossy?"

"I don't think she's that type."

Marianne reacted with an echoing, condescending laugh.

"That's pretty obvious, Victoria."

The Press Queen's words faded into lip movements spreading wide over coarse consonants. Her legs moved to every passionate twitch, encroaching too often into her retiring assistant's personal space.

Victoria smiled and nodded.

21.

Lillian enjoyed her journey home from work as a sort of alternate dimension; a place between lives where circumstance allowed a pause on reality. But today was different, like every other day after it would be. She was pregnant. Alone time was what she didn't need.

She walked slowly up Parliament Street towards Charing Cross Station, in sight of Trafalgar Square. Its fountain made her want to rush to its marbled edge. Tourists with long-lens cameras snapped like excited children in reaction to every stimulant: fat pigeons hopping for scraps, performance artists in weird clothes, flashes from other cameras. It was London; her second heartbeat. She had never considered a third.

She switched her phone off and walked homewards.

Down Charing Cross's steps, she snubbed an offer of an evening rag. Shock factor stories, she felt, would only weigh her down. In sustained resolve, she turned away from the shouting advertisements on the walls.

Peace. Please can I have some peace, London.

The light of an approaching Northern Line tube illuminated the dark tunnel, blowing in a breeze that lifted skirts and messed up perfect hairstyles. Enviously, she looked on at wannabe supermodels and wished that unmanaged hair was her biggest problem.

She settled into a fold-down seat at the top of the carriage and people-watched. Everyone in London was free to be as mad as the thoughts in their head, she thought. One girl wore a costume red bow in her blue hair; presumably to clash with her purple dungarees.

She came from Camden, Lillian thought, too wearied to develop her analysis further.

"STAND BACK FROM THE PLATFORM," a TFL steward shouted into her ear. She dismounted the carriage in a haze to catch her connecting train.

"WAIT FOR THE NEXT TRAIN! PLEASE ALLOW PASSEN-GERS ROOM TO GET OFF THE TRAIN!"

She waited for the next one. More alone time.

"Phil! Phil! I'm here! Over here."

She threw her arms up over her head.

"Hey, you!"

'Hey back at you! This never happens!'

"No, but it was bound to at least once."

"I guess so, Professor Hawking."

He smiled and kissed her forehead.

"How are you?"

"Good. Better now that you're here. And you? How's the case going?"

"Great actually. Debbie phoned in sick, which was a real pain at first, but then dug up a cracker of a precedent. From home! Imagine that for dedication?"

"Oh ya? But she's just the secretary isn't she?"

Phil sensed her jealousy and played on it.

"Well Ray's actually going to support her through Law School—give her an apprentice. She researches for us on some cases."

Lillian tried to hide her green eyes.

"She's married, Lillian! Come on, stop being such a girl."

"I don't know what you're talking about."

"You're such a little girl sometimes, do you know that?"

A smile forced its way onto her face.

"That's why you love me. So what else happened today?"

"Dad called, he's coming to visit on Saturday."

He studied her face for a sign of disappointment and found it.

"What's your problem with my dad, Lillian?"

"Nothing. He's just a bit…arrogant at times."

"And your dad is perfect?"

He paused. She hoped to retract.

"Honest to God, you spend all your time with your head in your pop psychology books and then you can't even notice your childish behaviour. What's the point of it all?"

As if he gets to lecture me on emotional self-control.

"Be nice to my dad, Lillian. That's all I'm saying. I'm nice to yours."

"I really couldn't give a DAMN about my father. He doesn't feel, Philip. You know that."

"Oh here we go—load us both down with your deepest, darkest issues and make it all into a massive drama about *you*. Change the record."

His words rattled her into silence. After half an hour's tension, they reached the door of their apartment.

"Listen, I'm sorry. I said a bit much. But I'm not getting into this. It's a bit heavy after a long day. Forget I said a thing."

She sat angry on the sofa and thought about how he hadn't even asked how her presentation went. Or if she had got her period.

He pounded around the apartment, chucking away the constrictions of his brief case and coat and kicked his shoes inconsiderately in front of the door.

"What's for dinner?"

That's IT.

She raced for the kitchen. He met her at the door.

"You're so self-absorbed you don't even realize how selfish you can be."

"Selfish?! Would you listen to yourself? I asked you to be nice to my dad instead of acting like a child. I pulled you for your behaviour because you needed to be pulled. Why does that have to turn into an episode of East-fucking-Enders?"

"I may have been rude to call him arrogant, which come on, let's face it, he is—but you didn't need to be so fucking condescending about *my* methods to keep myself happy—you crude *prick*. I'm trying to shed my issues. I *admit* to my shortcomings—*you* don't.

After the anger, the real emotion surfaced; still solid but less aggressive.

"I'm just trying to be a stronger person..."

His mood softened.

"I'm sorry, Lillian."

You should be.

"You know it's not easy for me. You of *all* people know what I've been through and how far I've come. And it's not pop psychology, you moron. It's neuro-science. I'm not sticking fairy tales to my mirror trying to delude myself about reality, for *God's sake*. I'm trying to understand myself...using a RATIO-NAL method of self-inquiry."

He bowed his head.

"I went too far. I know I went too far. I won't say sorry again."

Was she hearing things? Was he actually starting another argument? He wouldn't say sorry again?

"I'll just say that I'm going to pop down to Frank's and get us a nice dinner, maybe some mozzarella dippers to start...

His hand gently gripped hers.

...while you put your feet up and turn on the telly, or read your book—whatever makes my woman happy. We're just tense. When I come back we'll talk about what's *actually* bothering us."

"Fine."

She shivered at the thought.

Alone, she sat looking at their picture frames. The beautiful picture of them on the beach in Cornwall was taken after a row over money. They barely spoke all evening. But his friend Gene thought it would make a good snap. So they smiled as though they were happy. Now, every time people looked at it, they would think them a happy couple. Wasn't that the point—to convince others how happy they were; to put up a façade of fulfilment while ignoring unsettling feelings of emptiness? There was so much deceit in an average person's life, she was beginning to see. She was being deceitful this moment, hiding her pregnancy.

She looked at the photo of her and Stephen and welled up.

"I hava de fooda for the lady bella."

Phil's return took her by surprise.

"You're just missing the rose between your teeth, you cheese ball."

"The lady haza good nose for da cheesa. I hava mozzarella in battered balls righta here."

'OK, Phil.'

Just be quiet and put the food on the plates.

"Fancy some red wine?"

"Yes."

As he tilted the bottle towards her glass she blocked it with her hand.

"Actually, maybe we should lay off the booze tonight. We've a lot to talk about."

"Oh, right. I'll just get the plates."

"Finally."

She had meant to say it in her head.

What was she muttering? And why? He had apologised, made it up to her and done his best to crack a smile out of her. Was this what she considered a commensurate repayment?

They sat at the table.

"So, Lillian, what's really wrong?"

His face looked to her like a parent pacifying a moody teenager.

"Phil, don't do this. Don't do what you always do and turn it around to look as though I started this. You were looking for something to argue over tonight. You're father was just a smokescreen. I know there's something else. Just spit it out."

She knew everything. She was never wrong. Not Lillian.

"I'll say it again, you *are* rude to my father and yes, it puts me off you at times—especially because you go around acting like Miss Nice all the time."

"Here we go, keeping the old argument going, not getting anywhere. Phil, you were weird last night, too. It doesn't take a rocket scientist. You're mad because I'm going to Vietnam. Everything else is just horse shit."

Was she really saying those words? she asked herself, puzzled. Why had she spoken those words?

"I'm not. I told you I understand that you have to go—and watch your language. This doesn't have to get so heated."

"Oh get real, Phil. Parenting me like that. Do you really think I can't see what you're doing?"

"Please, Doctor, tell me what I'm doing? What are the tell tale indicators from my behaviour that I'm manipulating the truth?"

"That sarcasm is beyond immature. And if you must know, you're using textbook self-preservation. Now grow up."

She grated her chair against the tiles on her way up.

"So you're just walking away?"

"Yes, I am. Because I have no intention of entertaining any more of this. You either admit to what's eating you or we stop talking."

Was she really being that psychotic? she asked herself, unable to understand the character now controlling her tongue.

"Enjoy your dinner."

She sat on the sofa, surrounded again by framed smiles and colour.

Phil replayed the argument in his head, twirling his fork around and around the spaghetti. She was right. He was afraid. Long distance was hard and he wasn't sure if he was up to it anymore.

22.

Lillian bolted upright. Her alarm, a birthday gift from an old college friend, was fog-horn loud.

'GOOD MORNING BALTIMORE, EVERY DAY'S LIKE AN OPEN DOOR.'

She thumped it silent and lay in bed. She hadn't heard him leave. He wanted it that way, she figured; since he hadn't given her a goodbye kiss. What a way to make things worse. Sleeping on an argument was about the most dangerous thing they could have done.

'MARIANNE CALLING'

"Hello?"

"Yes, hello. I need you to meet me at Barbican station at 8:30. We have a meeting with a representative from UN Development fund on Greater Sutton Street. I tried calling you a dozen times yesterday evening."

"Development fund? Why? I thought our only concern with the UN was our application to the Committee for NGOs?"

"Yes, of course, consultative status. But this meeting is a *networking* opportunity. The person we're meeting is a nice guy, a friend of my father's. We'll learn something."

"OK, but you could have told me about this yesterday."

"You left the office after roasting Scott and switched your phone off."

"It wasn't off. I just..."

Marianne rushed to stop her.

"I'm not really bothered. Are you coming?"

"I'll meet you outside the station."

"Fine."

Lillian had research and soul-searching to do. She hadn't finished her lesson plans or summarised how the UN Convention on the Rights of the Child related to Vietnam. She hadn't picked up a Lonely Planet. She hadn't found a place to live.

Trust Marianne to push me into things.

There was plenty of time for 'networking,' she sighed, wiping cleanser to her face.

She put on her jacket a few minutes later and turned the key in the door.

Life. Is. Good.

She repeated the words over and over. Deep breaths slowed her thoughts down. Meeting a UNICEF representative might actually be helpful, she thought. And it might even send her research in a better direction.

Which way to Barbican?

She stood in front of a framed plan of the city's rail and underground channels, Chai tea late in one hand, the index finger of the other running along mazes.

Either Eastbound on the Jubilee to Westham then switch for the Hammersmith and City to Barbican. No, too many stops. Jubilee to London Bridge? Change for Northern Line to Moorgate—just one stop from Barbican?

Hmmm. . .To Westham!'

Did I just say all of that out loud?

How embarrassing.

She spun round to see if anyone was within earshot. A TFL guy looked at her. Her gaze dilated in fear.

"Alright, Love?"

Is-he-asking-me-that-because-I-looked-at-him-or-did-he-actually-hear-me-talking-to myself? Dear God, the neuroticism's taking over. I'm-going-to-become-one-of-those-people-on-the-tube-who-talk-to-themselves.

Just turn and walk.

As she walked on, silently thinking along the lines of: *well if he had said this then I would have said that,* she stumbled upon sense and calmed down. She walked to the platform, reached into her bag and took research notes out. Her mind settled onto the pages, too busy for now to cause more trouble.

An article from Time Magazine told of HIV-positive kids shunned from a Vietnam School.

> *'For two years, the Ho Chi Minh City Orphanage had been lobbying to enrol 15 HIV-positive children in a public primary school. . .When the day finally came; other parents who had been informed ahead of time about the new arrivals grabbed their children. . ., loudly making it known that they would never allow their children to be there while the 'infected' children were. . .One of the children cried and said: 'They drove us away. . . They hate us.'*

This can't continue, Lillian boomed.

> *'A 70-year-old woman, said: 'We survived the French bombings and the American bombings. I'd rather be bombed to death than die slowly of AIDS.'*

How can people be this ignorant?

'The irony in this case is that Vietnam has some of the most sweeping HIV/AIDS laws in the world. Children cannot be barred form school because they or any of their family members have HIV/AIDS. The law also states that employers cannot fire nor can doctors refuse to treat anyone because of their HIV status. Even the laws in the United States are not as far reaching.'

She paused to digest and read on.

'In Vietnam, most of the estimated 300,000 people who have AIDS are intravenous drug users, sex workers or their children. Its association with 'social evils' makes it tough to combat the myths and ignorance around AIDS.'

The train reached Westham. Lillian ran across the platform to meet the approaching Hammersmith and City train, squeezed her way into a seat and reached for fresh pages. A UNICEF report drew her in.

'More than half of the country's HIV cases are among people between 20 and 29 years of age, while one in every ten HIV-positive persons is under 19. . .It is estimated that 300,000 children are affected by AIDS in Vietnam'.

She committed the facts to memory before throwing the tattered notes into her bag. Marianne was standing outside Barbican station searching the crowd.

"Over here! We're late. It's 8:40."

Lillian refused to run in heels and stubbornly kept a steady gait.

It might piss her off, she thought, *which wouldn't be such a terrible consequence.*

"Good morning, Marianne. How are you?"

Lillian figured she might as well start out nice.

"Fine. The meeting's at 9. I thought I'd give us time to find the place. We don't have as much time now as I initially planned. We better get going."

"I'm sure we'll find it in plenty of time, Marianne. Which street did you say again?"

Listen to her giving false assurances, Marianne raged inside. *How could she possibly know if we have enough time or not? She doesn't even know the street name. What a flake.*

"Leave the navigating to me. I took the time to Google map it."

Of course you did. How did anyone ever get where they were going before Google Maps?

"Lead the way so, boss."

"The guy is a friend of my father's. There's nothing official about this meeting *per se* but we should really be looking to make an impression."

She was incurable. As if the UN guy gave a shite about anything other than his own ambition, Lillian thought.

"I'm sure he's just going to want to talk about the issues we'll need to tackle in Vietnam."

"Obviously. But there are other things we could do with knowing, like which benefactors are most interested in Vietnam. This is a fundraising opportunity, too."

"Alright."

Marianne asked the building receptionist to phone her contact.

"Ricky! He's just gone out actually. Can I leave a message?"

Marianne did her best to sublimate the physical manifestations of her erupting fury. Lillian saw it bubbling and bit her lip to keep from laughing.

"No thank you."

Lillian approached Marianne delicately.

"Do you have his mobile number? Maybe you could give him a call and see where he is? I'm sure he's just popped out."

Marianne's claw dug its way into her delicate pink Chanel bag for her iphone.

"Ricky, Marianne here. We have a 9am meeting."

Poor Ricky, Lillian thought.

"We'll be there in ten."

"We'll be where in ten?"

"Starbucks. He's having an 'espresso.' It's 9-bloody-am and he's having Starbucks."

Marianne became aware she was putting on a show for Lillian.

"We need to get to Clerkenwell road. It's five minutes from here."

Lillian spotted their contact through the window: tall, wearing specs, alone, and reading *The Economist.*

"That's got to be him, Marianne."

Marianne pushed the doors open and abruptly introduced a lagging Lillian.

"Ladies! I'm so sorry. I've been in the office since 7. I just popped out for a break. I thought you two were coming at 9:30."

"No. Nine."

Lillian steered the conversation to give Marianne time to recover her adulthood.

"Not to worry. We're all here now. So, have you been to Hanoi before, Ricky?"

Ricky. Is. Gorgeous.

"No. But I'm informed about it. I hope I can be of use to you both."

His smile revealed perfect white teeth.

"I'm sure you will. I was just reading about AIDS on the tube this morning. There seems to be a serious need for a decent information campaign."

He perked up.

"Absolutely. There's a lot of misinformation surrounding the issue. UNICEF Vietnam is working on it but there's a lot left to do. It's great that you guys are interested in that. Will you be dealing with nutrition issues too? And the increase in fatal accidents?"

"Not right away, though of course we intend to. Can you speak a bit about it?"

"Sure. Where to start! Well, we're working to ensure that birthing mothers are given information about neonatal mortality and post-natal nutrition. There's a serious problem in that regard, especially among the ethnic minorities. They just don't have the information. In one province, the mortality rates are alarming, something like 63 deaths per 1,000 births. That's four times the national average..."

Lillian was impressed.

...we also need to do more to ensure farming families get the greatest harvest out of their crops. But they're suspicious and adopting new farming techniques can be an issue for them."

"That's interesting. I'll definitely look into that. What about the accidents? Why are they happening?"

"You'll see why the moment you walk the streets of Hanoi. The traffic is horrendously anarchic. One scooter often carries families of four. Children rarely wear helmets or belts. It's madness."

He sighed as he relayed the information, running his hands through his wavy blonde hair.

"And the rest happen by drowning, mostly during the floods, and on farms; where children from poor families are expected to work from a young age."

Marianne grew bored and cut to the chase.

"So, Ricky, who do you think we should be targeting in terms of our fundraising campaign? I mean, besides the public. Do you know of any guilty rich people or donators with a special interest in Vietnam?"

He laughed a loud I-can't-believe-she's-just-asked-me-that laugh.

"I'm probably the worst person to speak to in that regard. Ask me anything about the political and economic situation over there, but not that!"

Her face dropped.

"Ricky, thank you for your time."

"No problem, Marianne. Tell your father I asked for him."

"Sure."
Lillian traded numbers with Ricky and followed Marianne to the tube.

84

"What a waste of time."

"It wasn't really. I'm sure I can use him to make contacts in Hanoi. I thought it was well worth it actually."

Marianne responded with a barely audible grunt.

Lillian used the tube time to write up another to-do list.

It's only a few weeks away. I need to get my jabs, my visa and what the fuck will I pack? Where will I live? What about language basics?

She felt a nerve snake wriggle around the pit of her stomach.

This is really happening.

Grande coffee was a bad idea.

❧

"Richard, we-haven't-thought-this-through. How-are-we-realistically-going-to-manage-our-operations-over-there-without-an-office? What-are-the-regulations-for-foreigners-renting-accommodation? You-don't-expect-me-to-sort-everything-out-alone?"

Richard laughed.

"Of course I don't. I've been taking care of the paperwork. I really need to sit down with you and explain the legal frameworks."

"Yes, you really do."

"No time like the present."

Richard reached for a folder and rolled up his sleeves.

"Right, let's get started. So, Lillian, you're visa is being sorted and you are fully entitled to rent whatever residential accommodation you please in Hanoi. You also have permission to set up a bank account for our expenditure account. From today, you'll need to make contact with Vietnam's committee for foreign NGOs and the People's Aid Coordinating Committee. I have contact details here for the people you will be dealing with. By law, we have to send reports every six months about our operations there. But they'll be sniffing you out quite a bit when you first arrive; probably asking you to report to them regularly. They'll want you to provide documentation whenever they request it, too. No questions asked. Just co-operate with them. In time, we'll get them on our side...

Why don't I know this already?

...It's nothing to worry about. But since you are our chief representative, you will be accountable for everything. They already have your CV and details about your background. I will need a copy of your passport though. They require that."

You will be accountable for everything.

The sentence slapped her face.

"So...am...I just need to focus on our core objectives. Can I start by co-ordinating the distribution of aid in the provinces? And, I can't believe I don't know this, who are our suppliers going to be?"

"I'll go over that with you, too. Don't worry, it's all been taken care of. You will need to liaise with the people's committees in the various provinces as you do everything. By law, they are supposed to support you, but they will probably be wary of you at first. Just make contact with them, speak to them of our intentions and we'll start sending out the troops, so to speak...

...have a look at the New Hanoian online for places to rent. Alternatively, I can get Lydia from admin to sort a place out for you."

"Lydia, ask Lydia."

"Are you sure you're OK with this? I mean, you did go to Guatemala last year."

Do I not look OK?

"Of course. I just have a lot to organise."

"If you need time off, just ask."

"Can I take the rest of today?"

"Sure. Go for it. Do what you have to do."

Lillian made for the fire escape. Its privacy offered her the space she needed to cry.

What am I doing? Am I keeping this baby?

"Honey, what's wrong? Are you crying?"

Tears blocked her nose, her vision and her every other sense.

Why did I call him?

"No. Yes. But I'm fine."

"Baby if this is about last night, I'm sorry. Don't worry, we can sort it out."

"I'm just really afraid, Phil."

"Hey, it's OK. I love you. Nothing is going to come between us. Do you hear me? You were just being a brat last night."

He laughed and urged her to do the same.

"It's no big deal, alright?"

"Ya."

"I'll be home early. Just settle for now, OK?"

"OK."

She was alone on the fire escape with sadness, an emotion she grappled with. Sadness, to her, was associated with coffins and smoky incense. To avoid pain and dark memories, she would replace tears with self-directed anger—for giving in to weakness. On the tube, she allowed sadness its time and took solace in her anonymity.

She thought about Stephen. He was seven, she was nine. It was her fault, no matter what people said. It was *her* responsibility to make sure he got home from school safe. He was too small to walk behind. She had wanted to talk to her friend without him listening in and didn't notice him cross the road into a car.

It was as though time froze. The sounds still made her shake; the screech of the ambulance siren, screaming neighbours running out of their houses. The memory of Stephen's blood on the road would forever haunt her, as would the guilt of doing nothing but watch her urine spill down the side of her leg. She reached her bed and fell into old, familiar nightmares.

"Sweety, it's me. What's wrong? Are you OK? You're drenched."

"Where am I?"

"Honey, wake up."

"I said *don't*. . ."

"Lillian, wake up."

"Stephen?"

"No, sweetie—it's me, it's Phil."

"Oh."

"Honey, it's OK. *Please* stop letting things build up to this."

Lillian took the glass of water out of Phil's hand.

"I just don't see the point in sharing misery. I can't control my dreams but I can control my emotions."

There was no point talking to her when she got like this, Phil thought. None at all.

"I love you. Lillian, I love you completely. You can't lose my love. Do you know that?"

Of course she could lose it, she thought. Even the love of a parent wasn't certain—and that, apparently, was life's greatest guarantee.

"Yes. I do. I know."

Phil pulled her in. No one could protect her from herself the way he could.

23.

It was Saturday and Lillian's haze hadn't lifted. She shrugged off her date with Jessie and retreated into a mild depression.

Am I keeping the baby?

"Lillian, dad'll be here in a few."

"OK."

It's so not OK.

Dominic knocked first and walked in. The sight of what Lillian considered a pretentious dress code altered her chemistry.

"Hello, Mr Sutcliffe."

"Dominic, please call me Dominic."

Can't he just give up?

"Right."

He shoved his coat into her hand, reinforcing her belief that he was indeed a chauvinist pig.

I have a vagina so I'm happy to wait on him hand and foot. Is that it?

Phil greeted his 'chief' with a rough handshake. Lillian rolled her eyes, hung his coat on the stand and made her way to her place in the kitchen. She watched them through the French shutters while preparing tea.

Phil's dad's gut is the size of a full-term pregnancy.

Pregnancy. Full term.

Snap out of it.

She diverted her attention to his baby finger; to his gold ring.

Only men with superiority complexes wear those.

She walked toward father and son with a tray. Today was about being nice, with sugar lumps and cookies and china.

"LILLIAN!"

His voice rolled like thunder through their small apartment.

"You're leaving my boy again!"

In theory, she thought, the after-shock of his roar was powerful enough to 'accidently' knock the tray from her hands onto his lap. She thought better of capitalising on the clear opportunity.

"Yes, I leave for Vietnam in a few weeks."

"Always off saving the world! Where were you the last time?"

She had told him a thousand times.

"*Guat-em-a-la.*"

"Oh yes, now I remember. You were gone for bloody *months.*"

"I was gone for two months, Mr Sutcliffe."

Name calling was a good weapon.

"Please, Lillian. Don't call me that, it makes me feel old."

And the balding hair doesn't?

"And who's going to mind you, Phil? I suppose you'll have more time to spend with your brothers. You'll be able to come on the hunts with us again, too.'"

Phil threw a meek glance Lillian's way.

"Oh, I forgot myself," Dominic let out, hand pressed to his mouth. "You'll have to excuse me Lillian. You must think me very crude."

If only you knew.

'It's OK.'

She choked back the anger, for Phil.

"I knew you weren't as serious as he said you were, dear. After all, 'tis a fun sport. Christ, you'd think we were torturing the bloody things."

"A pack of sixty dogs terrorising one fox is fun? While men on horseback shout orders to *kill*? Personally, I think there are better ways to have fun."

She avoided Phil's eyes.

"We're not going to agree on this one, Lillian."

He turned to Phil and stirred the sugar in his cup.

"So, Philip, tell me about this big important celebrity case? Have you cracked it yet?"

Lillian sat quietly, trying to drown out the legal speak.

It's enough to turn a raging insomniac into Rip-Van-fucking-Winkle.

Like a true warrior, she smiled and nodded her way through three hours of nauseating grandiloquence.

"I'm sorry he stole our afternoon, pretty. You know what he's like."

"It's fine. Let's go. I have a doctor's appointment."

Be brave, be brave. The doctor can tell him, the doctor can tell him.

"Can't you do that alone?"

Yes, and I can raise the fucking child alone too.

"I suppose. I just thought it'd be nice to get out and get some air. You know, together."

"It would, but now that I've started to think about the case I can't stop. I really fancy doing some research. Isn't that OK?"

"Sure. Of course it is."

"Are you being sarcastic?"

"Never.'

She closed the door and blew the tightness out. She hadn't told her mother she was going to Vietnam. Or that she was pregnant. Or that she was hiding it hoping it would go away. Or that she was considering, she couldn't say it: ab...

She sat on a bench and dialled.

She'd start with Vietnam.

24.

It was Lillian's last day at the office. She was still pregnant, despite her use of the law of repulsion. She sat at her desk and flicked through a guide book on Vietnam. The language looked impossible.

'The French got rid of the enigmatic character system and replaced it with the Roman alphabet; a tyrannical move, but one that Westerners appreciate. It is mono-syllabic, with six tones represented by symbols with functions we may compare to the accent grave used in French—or the fada in Irish.'

Com-plex.

'One word spelled the same could mean any number of things depending on the symbol's place—under of over the letter, pointed up or down, left or right.'

Is there any point in trying?

The photographs of Vietnam made it look like something out of a history book. Buffalos were tractors and double-ended basket poles freight carriers. One photo showed a pig tied to the back of a Honda scooter, the army-helmeted driver gripping a cigarette with his teeth.

Her mind drifted inwards.

Phil hadn't noticed a thing. He was too busy with that case he couldn't stop thinking about. His preoccupation with it, Lillian convinced herself, was why they hadn't talked much lately, about anything—her leaving, him staying. Pregnancy.

But, she consoled herself, she'd be back in three months—*exactly* when people chose to announce pregnancies. Perfect, really.

Am I having the baby, then?

Maybe.

25.

Richard had been sweet enough to hire vegetarian caterers and a high-brow venue. Lillian looked up at gilt-edged leaves decorating the borders of the dome-shaped hall and smiled. She wore a fitted floor-length silk dress while she still had the figure.

Her roving eyes stalled on Phil and Guy. She willed Phil to meet her gaze from across the room, using the mysterious force that informs two intimate people of the other's mere intention. Phil turned his head and met her eye. She smiled, inviting him to do the same. He accepted with eyes that had lost their sparkle. Acknowledging the tension at this point, she felt, would mean leaving awkward ripples.

She headed for the bar alone and thought seriously about tequila. Quickly, she reminded herself of the company she was in and the company that was in her.

She made her way to Jessie.

"Great leaving party, Lils! So, how *are* you?'

"Fine...ish. I know Phil's miserable. I hope he can deal with this."

"He can; he is. And will. Just enjoy this. He's going to miss you, no big deal. It's totally normal. In fact," Jessie said, her eyes widening dramatically, "it's the oldest running show on Broadway: lover goes away, other lover gets sad. I'd be worried if he *wasn't* feeling miserable."

"True that. OK you've earned you're reward. Let's show you off to Guy."

"Let's."

Jessie messed her hair up the way she liked it as she strolled in faux-coolness across the room. Lillian tried not to meet the stares of guests drawing her into conversations and failed. Jessie walked on.

"Sorry, Jess!"

"Don't be. Go on. But come back—I don't do awkward silence very well."

"Are you sure you've met Guy?"

Hours passed. Lillian walked to drunk Phil, directing her dirtiest look at Guy and Jessie for leaving him alone all night.

"Honey, I mizzed you."

His eyes drooped in depression.

"So did I, honey. I tried to get away. You know what it's like."

Phil's ability to mask his emotions had disappeared with his sobriety.

"Let's take you outside for a bit?"

"OK, Lilly Poo...oo...zz."

Lilly what? Lillian thought. *That's new. And creepy.*

They walked outside onto a perfect lawn. Tiny lamps lit up the borders of the garden pathways. She took his hand in hers and led him to the gazebo.

"Can you believe I'm leaving tomorrow?"

Phil looked at the ground and followed an imaginary car around a grid.

"Yezzz."

Yes, what does he fucking mean, Yes? I'll give him yes.

"Richard gave me a lovely gift. Look—it's a gold necklace. And it has a compass built in—so I'll always know which way home is. How corny is that?"

"ver nizzz."

What an asshole getting drunk on my last night.

"Maybe we should get a taxi home. It's late."

"Hhhhhhhhhhhh....how come you weren drin-kkk-in?"

Because I'm pregnant, you shit. And now you're hiccupping. Nice.

"I have to get up early. Come on, let's go."

Lillian attempted to disguise that she was an irritation away from violence. In gritted-teeth determination, she smiled on the receiving end of dozens of drunken sumo hugs.

I so can't do tears right now.

"Ah, Jess. Don't. We have Skype and webcams and instant messaging. There's no need. Do you hear me?"

"I know, it's just that...I'm..."

It's just that you're fucking drunk and nothing else.

"I'm going to miss you so much."

I'm a horrible person.

"I'll miss you too. Give me a hug."

"Promise you'll mind yourself out there."

"I promise."

"OK. Xhin Ciao!

'Xhin what?'

'Xhin...Ciao? As in—hello and goodbye in Vietnamese?'

"Oh. Yeah. Xhin Ciao."

Lillian closed the door of the taxi and wondered why she didn't know her basic greetings. Phil's head moved to the will of the driver's wheel.

26.

"Lillian, it's NOON!"

"JESUS CHRIST! Did you turn off my alarm?"

"Did you set it?"

"Oh God," she screamed, springing from the bed.

"I need to be in Heathrow in *three* hours. My packing's not finished. My fucking packing's NOT finished."

She hyperventilated and forced her mouth into speech.

"Phil, get your ass in gear NOW. There's a list on the kitchen counter. Go to the pharmacy and get *everything*. GO."

"OK, drill sergeant."

"Oh fuck you and your digs! Just go!"

Phil threw on clothes and ran for the safety of the door.

Lillian catapulted herself out of the room and willed her legs to get her to the living room in four strides. She ran with knees up, hurtling past obstacles, battering her knee against the edge of a chair. She howled at the ceiling and thought seriously about confronting the chair.

OH HOLY MOTHER OF GOD!!!

It's fine. It's fine. If I give myself an hour, I'll be there in time.

Phil burst in the door like a tornado twenty minutes later, falling pathetically over the shoes in front of it.

Karma, Lillian thought—*for all those times you kicked your shoes there without caring.*

He looked slowly up at Lillian in her wiry hair and knickers and exploded into laughter. She joined in, squawking at the pitiful sight of him. He stood up to reveal he had put her pink t-shirt on inside-out and back-to-front. The soles of her yellow flip-flops finished before his heel.

"Phil! Why? *Why* are you dressed in me?"

Her shoulders hopped up and down in laughter.

"I panicked."

"You don't say!"

"Look who's talking, Woody Allen."

"How could we let this happen?"

"Let's just get on with it. No hows or whys. We just did. Now be quiet. My head's thumping."

Phil put her first aid essentials into the small case he had just bought her. It wasn't on the list, he thought, but should have been. She never thought of the finer details. How would she manage without him? He made a mental note of the things she would likely forget—webcam, phone charger, torch and so on. He started to gather them, which took longer than it should have. She had a place for nothing.

She watched him from the living room noticing what he was doing for her, even though she knew he wouldn't recognise that she did.

Watching Phil in her clothes, putting all his effort into making sure she would have everything she needed, she felt the familiar lump in her throat.

"Phil, I need to get dressed. Then we leave. Can you try to zip up my suitcase?"

"I should be able to, yes—if I press the fridge down on it for a minute or so."

He winked at her. She didn't notice.

"I don't even have time for a shower."

Hardly the end of the world, Phil thought.

"Just put on some de-rodent. Should keep the pong at bay for a while."

Lillian laughed and accepted his recommendation. They were both avoiding seriousness.

❧

Phil had taken care of everything: taxi, bag drop—saving a scanned copy of her passport to her laptop. "Just in case anything should happen," he had said when she asked him why.

The remaining passengers were called over the public announcement system. Lillian's heart beat in her chest. Her mind sped off with thoughts of grief.

"Phil...I love you."

The unwelcome invader got the better of her, making its way up to her eyes. There were floods and nostril flares and other physical symptoms of trying, but failing, to hold back heartbreak.

"This will be the last time..."

It was a lie, he well knew. But he loved her anyway.

Man, do I love her.

"You're my woman and I love you. Get home to me soon, you hear me?"

She buried her head in his chest.

"Hey, don't. It's OK. Go, Lillian. You better go. They're calling again. You don't have time."

She kissed his cheek and walked away without turning back. He watched until the doors closed. She was gone with his heart again.

27.

The cells in Lillian's body vibrated with life. She was hyper aware, with all the jitters and twitches and quivers that epic adventures bring. As she looked around the Korean Airlines flight from Seoul, she noticed she was the only white person on board.

What's happening? Am I really flying to Hanoi? Alone? Where I know nobody?

Destination Hanoi. Hanoi. I'm on my way to Ha——noi.

She spun it in her mind, trying to make it familiar.

Best to just stay in the safety of the present moment, she thought.

Because, even if I tried to, how could I possibly imagine what the next few hours will have in store?

She was creating new neural pathways in her head; changing her brain circuitry with the potency of new experience.

Why all the fear?

She understood that it was foolish to fear the unkown. There was no rational frame of inquiry to follow. The unkown was simply that—the unkown. Who could predict if it would be good or bad? It could be either, or none, one or the other, or both. Worrying was pointless. It had no purpose whatsoever. But knowing and feeling were two very different things, and as she sat in her reclined seat, she quaked until touchdown.

A concert?

In genuine curiosity, Lillian waited for the parted doors to verify her suspicions. Not a concert; a sea of wrestling Vietnamese taxi drivers.

"Mademoiselle! Taxi! Taxi"

Men waved their arms above their head. Others tried to take her suitcase from her. Unhinged human behaviour on this scale was frightening...and fascinating. *Yes*, she told herself, *fascinating, not frightening.*

She spotted her name on a board.

A small Vietnamese man gave her a reticent handshake and a smile that revealed brown, irregular teeth. He introduced himself as Nguyen Thang Long and walked briskly to his car; an old, battered Honda.

The driving started.

Beeeeeeeeeeeeeeeeeeeeep.

Why is he beeping?

He overtook a car.

Beeeeeeeeeeeeeeeeeeeeep.

Huh?

A car overtook him.

Beeeeeeeeeeeeeeeeeeeeep. Beeeeeeeeeeeeeeeeeeeeep.

Huh?

A man lay face-down at the side of the road beside a tipped over motorbike. Traffic passed by.

Huh?

"We need to stop for that man back there, didn't you see him?"

The driver smiled in the rear view mirror, as if to accuse her of naivety.

She felt as though she had travelled through time into the past, that she had stepped into another realm; a place where the space-time continuum didn't operate as in the rest of the world. Through the dark, she glimpsed poverty, filth; chaos. Vietnam was like nothing she had experienced. Analytical mental frameworks that provided for environmental comprehension didn't seem to work for her in Vietnam.

Maybe they're not all as tough as Mr what's his face, she thought, desperately hoping it wasn't normal for a taxi man to catapult luggage from the boot of a car to a hotel door.

What is he doing?

Huh?

The unfriendly taxi man abandoned her lopsided suitcase on the broken concrete slab masquerading as a roadside pathway. He stood tall, stuck out his hand for payment, crunched the notes into his pocket and sped off in his creaky Honda. The four star hotel to the right of the luggage crime scene was an even mix of dilapidated shack and construction site.

I'm. . .scared.

A spiky-haired teenage boy in flip-flops bounced towards her. His face said "I just woke up. This is bothering me so we're going to get it over with as fast as is humanly possible. No questions."

The bumpy mattress on the lobby floor where the teenager had been sleeping almost tripped her over. He pushed past her, knees bent from the strain of the weight of her luggage, and signalled with his eyes for her to follow him to her room.

"Do you have internet?"

Spiky-haired boy stared back at her, smiling.

"Do you have internet?"

Spiky-haired boy smiled again.

Lillian typed the air.

"Internet, you know?"

Does he just think I'm doing my Gerry Lee Lewis impression?

The skinny teenager laughed out loud and turned for the door.

He does. Little prick.

What about Skype?

What about Phil?

How will he know I'm OK?

Shower. Just have a shower and chill out.

She opened the door to the bathroom.

Is that it?! A hose and a hole in the ground?!

She surrendered to circumstance and unopened a sachet of shampoo.

It's fine. This. Is. Fine.

The water ran cold on her skin.

This is not fine.

She thought about crying

Why am I here?

What am I doing?

I should be planning my new life. . .

She shivered her way to fully clothed, rested her head on the unfamiliar hotel pillow and began to slap pesky flies off her dry skin. She rummaged through her bag in search of insect repellent and found the first aid case Phil had packed for her.

Oh, Phil.

The small plastic box was filled with supplies Lillian didn't recognise. Comforted by her boyfriend's caring gesture, she drifted into sleep.

28.

An alien invasion of sound came through the open shutters in Lillian's hotel room. The unwelcome screech of chaotic traffic pierced through her brain. Two Vietnamese men chatted outside her room. The language they spoke was frightening, not fascinating, with a range of tones that made her feel out of her depth.

She dressed in a hurry, desperate to put a picture to the noise. In a first tentative attempt to cross a thin street, she was knocked to the ground by the back draft of a whizzing scooter.

What an asshole!

She scampered for the safety of a cockroach infested path. Her mouth hung open as she looked on, trying to understand the order. The scooters didn't stop for *anyone*, she soon realised. Across the street, a Vietnamese family laughed at her. Squatting in a circle over a naked flame, they laughed so hard they felt compelled to hold their abdomens. A medieval, decrepit house stood precariously behind them. The modern plastic toy furniture some of the adults sat on made it difficult for Lillian to distinguish between poverty and farce. Puzzled, she looked on at the ludicrous sight and wondered if she really was seeing grown-ups acting as though toy furniture was to be taken seriously.

And they're laughing at me?

Endless bands of revving scooters drove by without consideration for pedestrians. Lillian begun to understand what was expected of her: courage. Courage to walk out in front of traffic. She crossed her fingers and hoped her courage would be rewarded with safety. Her purple linen skirt blew in the traffic breeze. Her adrenaline pumped in pints.

Don't stop, don't stop, don't stop

With gritted teeth, she urged herself to follow protocol, despite everything in her makeup telling her it was suicide.

Don't do it.

Do it.

Don't do it.

Do it.

I made it!

She reached the tourist-and-French-designed heartbeat of the Old Quarter. Women in conical hats expertly negotiated traffic while carrying hanging fruit baskets on a poll. The haggard women collected around her, begging her to buy their exotic fruit. On close inspection, the women looked worn out and miserable. Their skin looked prematurely ridged, and the smiles on their faces meant nothing more than business.

"Em Oi, buy from me."

Em Oi?

She made a mental note to herself to write the phrase into the flowery notebook Phil had hidden in her carry-on bag. He had left a note with it recommending she write down the things she didn't yet know—'so she wouldn't forget to remember what she still had to learn.'

"I. Am. Sorry. But. I. Have. No. Dong."

How, Lillian wondered, could she better gesticulate what she was trying to say? The women looked deliberately confused, like they were playing a mind game with her. They followed her for blocks before accepting she wasn't catching their bait. In frustration, they spat some kind of insult. Lillian's pity for them waned a little.

The buildings around her were a paradoxical medley of Asian and French colonial architecture, with smatterings of makeshift buildings roofed in corrugated metal. Rows of beech trees decorated each street; their knotted roots breaking up through cracks in concrete footpaths. Multitudes of wires drooped at thoughtless levels from wooden electric beams. It was the most gaping public hazard Lillian had seen. An electric storm was not to be feared in Vietnam, she thought, sarcastically figuring it was because the country was anchored in an invisible layer of rubber that she, the sorest thumb in the city, couldn't see.

How is this normal?

Drains overflowed, collecting dirty water in sporadic puddles. Smoking glass-cased food stalls stood outside filthy homes on broken streets, offering dog meat, *Pho*, egg noodles and French baguettes to buyers mad enough to be tempted by it.

They eat dogs?

What's pho?

I need help.

Marianne had emailed contact details for a female translator whose profile, she said, had stood out. The woman described herself as French-Vietnamese and had interests apart from family and cooking. She had worked in the past as an air hostess for Vietnam Airlines and had travelled the world.

Her profile persuaded Lillian into thinking that she, 'Anh', had to be looser in herself than other, more reserved Vietnamese women. Plus, Lillian reasoned, since she would be spending a lot of time with her translator, a laid back personality was a prerequisite. She hurried back to the hotel and dialled her number.

"I be happy to. Meet me in Mao's Red Lounge at figh."

Anh's English didn't sound great, Lillian thought, figuring she must have meant *five*.

Lillian found Mao's near the back of the Old Quarter, on Ta Hien street. The bar was a tribute to the Communist dictator of the same name. Smiling Buddhas, t-pee candles and photos of drunken tourists stamped the bar in back-packer tack.

Anh stood from her seat at the bar.

"Hello! You must be: I try to say...Lee- lee—anne."

Her smile was huge.

"Yes. Hello! Ann?"

Anh laughed and threw her eyes to the ceiling.

" No. De H at end of my name sound like G in Enlish. My name soun' like dis: ANG. A...NG."

Lillian repeated it for Anh's approval.

Once satisfied, Anh initiated conversation.

"So, you will work for the shildren in Vietnam?"

"Yes. I. Will. Be. Starting. Work. On. Behalf. Of. My. Organisation. I. Will. Be. Leaving. For. Tanh Hoa. In. A. Few. Days. That. Will. Be. Our. First. Trip. Together. Is that OK?'

"Sure, you boss. You tell me and I go with you. No ploblem. But you not have to talk like I stupid."

Lillian felt her cheeks burn.

"I'm sorry. I just arrived. I'm just finding my feet."

"Is OK. So where you want live in Hanoi? You find apatment yet?"

"Gosh no. I wouldn't know where to start!"

"Gosh, what it mean?"

"I'm not exactly sure. It's just an...exclamation, I suppose."

"Like esslamation mack?"

"Yes, exactly."

"I learning a lot from you if I work with you. So you want live with me? I live myself in my sister's apatment."

Anh's facial expression didn't change with her forward offer.

"Do you have a spare room?"

"No. But we can buy mattess."

A base in Hanoi was really all she needed.

"Can I have a look at it?"

"Sewer."

"Ha!"

"What funny?"

"Do you know what a sewer is?"

I12

"No, what it is?"

"Never mind. I'll tell you later. But, can you please tell me: what does Em Oi mean?"

Anh smiled, proud to be asked about her culture's idiosyncrasies.

"*Em oi* is what you say when you want speak to young woman. And when you want speak to woman leetle oler, you say *Anh Oi*. It *Chi Oi* for an ol woman. It a way of speaking to people with the respect."

Lillian smiled at her response and shared similarities from the Irish language. They walked together to the narrow street outside, still chatting. Anh threw Lillian a spare helmet.

"You sit on back."

Anh slapped the seat of her white Vespa scooter a second time.

"Don't be scared. I good diver."

Lillian clung to Anh's small hips from the back seat, watching closely as she searched her huge leather bag in search of her keys. Chanel key rings dangled from the zip of Anh's bag and her clanking bunch of keys. She flicked the scooter stand off the ground and dragged the scooter into motion. Coolly, she set both feet down on the footrests and masterfully negotiated a sharp bend. Her slick confidence assured Lillian so much that she felt safe turning her attention to street theatre.

Male scooter drivers taxied mothers, who casually held young children in their arms. The entire safety code was based on confidence, or cockiness. A car bullied its way through a miniature street intersection like a fog horn's in an ants' nest, steamrolling through bustling traffic. Miraculously, passers-by remained uninjured.

Down side streets, mothers aired laundry; children played games with little balls of fire, prompting Lillian to remind herself to make a note of it her notebook. Old men played chess, or something like it. Everything seemed to be done in the open in Vietnam; life was a shared experience.

Anh slowed down at Dam Trau, a crowded apartment complex off a major ring road, within waking distance of the city centre.

This could work.

She took off her helmet and spotted rows of identical apartment blocks continuing for acres. Piled garbage burned at the end of each one. Groups of women in check shirts and conical hats heated their hands over the flames from tiny toy seats. The women watched Lillian dismount the bike in curiosity and suspicion. Lillian instinctively knew that, if she accepted Anh's offer, she would be the only foreigner in Dam Trau.

She traced the origin of contaminated water flowing under the curb in front of her, stopping to look at the woman in high heels and pyjamas Anh was greeting.

"She clean my clothes. If you live here, she clean your clothes too. Just 50,000 Dong. Figh dollar."

Lillian responded with a smile and followed her new friend into the apartment block. White walls were streaked in dirt art, doors hung open behind rusting iron bar gates; an aroma of decayed meat polluted all ten floors of the staircase. Like an old war movie, a tannoy crackled into life, startling Lillian.

"What is the man saying?"

"Oh, it stupid. He tell us be good citizens and love Vietnam. He think we stupid."

Lillian hadn't read about that level of propaganda in the guidebook, and silently berated herself for not taking Richard's advice about research.

"This it. You like?"

The toilet was immediately right of the kitchen entrance and stunk. A small window beside glass double doors separated the entrance from the rest of the apartment: an open plan living area. Multi-coloured butterflies painted onto the glass doors looked to Lillian like an amateur DIY job. The entire flat was no larger than a bedroom. The kitchen had no cooker or storage presses, just a fridge and a whitish tub standing on four rickety iron legs. Cracks on the wall tiles revealed a small colony of ants.

If it weren't for those shiny-white tiles, Lillian told herself, *I'd be running out of here.*

The white tiles covered the floors of the entire flat.

Love and light battling the dreary.

"Where would my mattress go?"

"Besigh TV. There space besigh the wall."

This is mad enough to work.

"I'll take it."

"I happy you say yes."

"Me too."

Lillian moved to hug Anh, who ignored—or failed to notice—the gesture.

"We get food now. I hungry. Then we get things fom hotel."

Lillian shrugged off the rejection and asked a final question.

"Yes. It wireless so you can use laptop."

And so it was.

29.

Phil was being cool on the phone. Did he think she wasn't finding it hard too? she had asked him; and Couldn't he *try* to show her support?

She got up from the dirty clay road she was squatting over and drank down the last of her bottled water. The sweaty mix of surging hormones and the Asian sun had been slowly baking her all day. She was cranky.

Why don't I just tell him?

"Leeleeane. It time," Anh shouted from the steps of the Committee Office.

"I'm Coming. Relax, woman. It's just a meeting."

"You should not be late at meeting. It roo."

"Alright. Jeeeze."

The Tanh Hoa Provincial People's Committee office was a tall brick building painted marigold yellow and red at the fringes. Outside, a Communist flag flew at full mast. The entire structure stood as an edifice; a vulgar bastion of authority, separated from the poor surroundings of the dusty city it stood over by high walls and iron gates. Much the same, Lillian thought, as a medieval castle's moat separated it from vagrants. It emitted a palpable air of impenetrability, a don-t-even-think-about-coming-near-me attitude of superiority.

Lillian, with the privileged status of guest, walked to its entrance and greeted a Vietnamese woman dressed in official uniform. She was determinedly serious and definitely, Lillian thought, not to be messed with. Jam jar lenses within square brown frames sunk her slightly crossed eyes far back into her skull. Her teeth were bucked and brown. She spoke in strict officialise, her back poker straight. Singlehandedly, she exploded to smithereens the sexist myth that all Asian women were affable and shy.

"The head of the committee and representative from foreign relations depatment will see you now."

She turned on her flat heels, smiled a crooked smile, and led the way to the meeting.

Lillian sat at the meeting table inside: a low-sized hand carved wooden antique. A painted teapot and tiny thimble cups were gathered within a round wooden tray at its centre. The walls were decorated in unframed water paintings of turtles and dragons. Wood-carved ornaments of flying phoenixes and rearing unicorns posed along the sills of each of the four windows. There were few trophies to the technological era, besides an old computer and a rotary dial phone.

A motley crew of uniformed and suited men smiled at Lillian as she looked around the room.

"Did you see statue of Le Loi in Tanh Hoa square?' the Committee Chairman asked her, reaching for the teapot.

"Yes, I did. Very nice."

She smiled, proud and satisfied that he had chosen to speak to her in English.

"You know who is he?"

"A warrior from the 14th Century, I believe."

"Yes? You tink?"

He smiled at his colleagues and spoke in Vietnamese. Laughter ensued.

"Le Loi was Emperor."

"Oh."

Lillian cringed and attempted a smile to thaw out her fear-frozen face. She followed it with a shoulder shrug in her best non-verbal expression of 'don't-mind-silly-little-me.'

"He won back the independence for Vietnam from China…"

"Oh."

"He is most honoured hero in Vietnam's history."

"Oh."

A long awkward silence rippled around the room. They were trying to expose her as a quack, a ditz, she feared.

"What else you know about our country? And why you choose Vietnam to help?"

Lillian had expected hostility, but not the inquisition. The Controller stepped in.

Emotion, bombard him with emotion.

"Sir, at Care about Children, our mission is to ensure that children all around the world get the basic needs they depend on for survival. My organisation chose Vietnam because we understand it is still getting to its feet after the war against the USA. We understand how much the country suffered, how it still suffers. We know that the effects of Agent Orange didn't end with the war and we want to do what we can to help. We have no political agenda whatsoever so, please, you will have to forgive me for my poor knowledge of your country's political history."

He paused and looked into her eyes, scouring them for honesty.

"You are only interested in the Agent Orange? Is that focus for the operations?"

"We have a few actually, Sir. I have a copy of the manifesto we sent as part of our application. Here, please take it."

"I trust you have met with NGO resource centre in Hanoi?"

"I have."

"And they will help you with the organisational issues?"

"Yes, Sir. They will help us hire Vietnamese staff."

He stood up and shook her hand.

"Vietnam is not suffering, Leeleeanne. Our country is growing strong."

"Yes, sir."

"The war is over."

And so was the meeting, finally.

30.

Geeky Gerard the German journalist smiled naively at Lillian's flirty taunts, believing them genuine. She had stage-managed their communication from the first email she sent him, flouting all respectable flirting mores to get her foot in. Ricky the UN guy, whom she had also led along a string, handed over Gerard's coveted details after no less than four emails—each way. Gerard worked for the press wire service and as a freelancer for an independent documentary company. He had contacts. Professional Lillian wouldn't have stood a chance. Single, made-up, cleavaged Lillian, however, would. A few complimentary nods to his work, which she 'just loved', and the mention—in her dizziest parlance—of being a woman alone in a frightening city, reeled him in.

They sat in an intimate corner of Duc's art-gallery-bar in Hanoi: the meeting centre of big egos masquerading as modest humanitarians.

Gerard was just about to film a major documentary and would be travelling to the South, he told Lillian. He planned to expose a Hanoi-based criminal circle trafficking women and young girls at the Cambodian border. He and his crew would be flying into Ho Chi Minh City the following week.

An eruption of courage spewed upwards into Lillian's mouth and morphed itself into an intelligible request.

"Can I come?"

Gerard looked at her, stunned by her frankness.

"But it will for sure be very dangerous, Lillian. If you think Hanoi is a challenge, I am not sure you are up for this."

He moved smugly towards his glass and poured dry whiskey back his throat.

She stared into his eyes.

"Please. You won't even know I'm there."

"But, Lillian..."

"No Buts, just say yes. You won't regret it. I just want to know the reality of the situation, and I want to know first hand. I can change lives with that knowledge. You know I can."

"I..."

"Just say it, Gerard."

"OK, yes, of course. How could I say no to those eyes?"

Gerard reached to brush her hair from her face. Lillian did her best to keep her skin from scurrying up the legs of the table in front of her.

31.

It was beanbag Sunday: a no-fuss, no-frills, easy-like-the-morning kind of day. Aromatic bubbles bounced around Lillian's mindscape, effortlessly snatching her unfocused attention from the jibberish Asian TV channels in front of her. Each spherical temptress bulged with delectable, sumptuous, mouth-titillating food, making their lonely little observer want to cry a little. What she wouldn't give, she sighed, for a salad baguette *or* creamy pasta *or* Belgian chocolate or *ooooooo*—potato fries with ketchup.

Binge-bridge here I come.

Her weak knees plodded her jelly legs down the steps of Dam Trau towards the nearest motorbike taxi. A mohawked man flicked away his cigarette a mili-second after catching her eye and trotted towards her with a spare helmet.

"Mademoiselle! Mademoiselle! Taxi! Taxi! Taxi!"

"Bao nhieu tien?" Lillian asked, staying calm and assertive, despite wanting to giggle in pride for remembering how to ask 'how much?' in the trickster language that was Vietnamese.

Surprised and disappointed, the taxi driver gave her the normal rate—and not the exorbitant rate gormless white people were charged.

Ha! I'm turning Vietnamese, I think I'm turning Vietnamese, I really think so, oh-oh-oh.

Her cheer unwittingly encouraged the slimers hanging out in the alley beside the local 'massage parlour.' In creepy-crawly chorus, they whistled and winked and gave all other manner of unwelcome verbal expression to their perverted minds. *Ick*, she thought, in veritable disgust. *I'm a pregnant woman.*

Together with Mr Mohawk, she whizzed off into the war-zone traffic and prayed to get to Pho Nha Tho Street in as few pieces as possible. Mr Mohawk stopped his engine abruptly outside a Cathedral, at a street intersection, and pointed Lillian to where she was going—a western café just West of Hoan Kiem lake.

"Cam on," she said to him in her freshest *bon mot*, before handing over a Ho Chi Minh emblazoned 20,000 Dong note—5,000 more than agreed.

"Cam on," he rebutted, impressed by her earnest efforts to play the game in his language. He beeped off into the crowded streets and left her to traipse around the perilous borders of the Old Quarter. She called for Anh.

"Meet me at Moca café?"

"Sewer."

"I really need to tell you what that means."

"What? What it means?"

"I'll tell you when you get there."

"I not forget dis time."

Anh rushed to Lillian's table and poked her in the back.

"Tell me. What it mean?"

"OK, sit down you crazy bitch."

"Beech? What dat mean?"

Lillian explained the rudimentary words to Anh while checking the menu for a vegetarian option.

Spring rolls, fries, baguettes. Yes, Please.

Anh gave Lillian's order to the waitress, who shared a laugh with Anh in Vietnamese.

"What did she say?"

"You hungry like pregnant woman."

Lillian hid her face behind the menu, let out a sheepish haaaa and diverted the conversation.

"So, tell me—were you born in Hanoi, Anh?"

"No, I bon in the noth; in countrysigh. I move to Hanoi after my mam die—when I twelve. She die because she sad. My brother die also. In de jail. He have AIDS. He did lot of drugs…

She bowed her head in an emotion Lillian tried to recognise.

"…People think you bad if you have de AIDS in Vietnam. Also, I a leetle French, so I not fully Vietnamese. My family sometigh ashamed. I not like so many Vietnamese girls and dey not like me."

It explained a lot, Lillian thought, gobsmacked she hadn't realised before that her friend had a dark story. She *was* different. Lillian could see it now. It was shallow of her to have assumed that Anh had simply bought into Western materialism. Vietnam had turned its back on her, which was why she hung out mostly with ex-pats. As she looked over the table at Anh's tumbling black locks, autumn eyes and soft, light-brown skin, she felt sad for her. A survivor like her didn't deserve ostracism as a reward.

"Vietnam is behind the times, Anh. You should never *ever* feel ashamed. You are an amazing person. You inspire me every day. I *bet* the rest of the world would say so, too."

"You not like Western girls. They all like flirt with the boys and drink lot of beer. One girl I live with from Germany, she always take my clothes and tell me lies. You diffent."

"What do you want from life, Anh?"

"A nice French boy."

"French? Only French?"

"Yes. My mam's dad were French."

"I wonder if there are French boys in here right now?"

Lillian ran her fingers through her blonde curls. She pouted at Anh, inviting her to get her best pose on.

"You so bad."

"And you so good—too good."

Lillian exploded into laughter realising she had involuntarily spoken like her new friend.

A mixture of English and Vietnamese; what would that be called? she thought to herself. *Venglish, maybe.*

Venglish, she decided, was her new language.

"Anh I speaking Venglish now. It English the way a Vietnamese person speak it."

"What it mean?"

The friendship was sealed.

32.

Pregnancy in Vietnam had to be the most unpleasant in the world, Lillian moaned, making a second attempt to open her eyes. Stifling heat, construction and noisy traffic chipped away at her peace, rattle by rattle. She snapped the shutters shut, groaning, and clattered her little toe against the edge of Anh's wardrobe. Red-faced and ire-fired, she tugged on the string of the crumby propeller-run air con.

I miss Phil.

The weight of a heavy heart pitying itself turned her walk into a grumbling trudge, and for every stride of the eight steps it took to get to the shower, she let out a deep sigh. To compound her mood; to really prove the law that negative thinking attracts negativity—the sewerage system had putrefied. Her early morning stomach vomited its bile in revulsion.

She skipped the shower and lay down instead on the mattress.

I miss Phil.

Anh had bought her a teddy—so she would '*stop talking about Phil.*' To justify the childish comfort she got out of it, Lillian told herself that squeezing an object into her torso would 'activate her parasympathetic nervous system' and thereby 'reduce anxiety.'

The teddy was about science, not her inability to cope alone. She wasn't, she assured herself, attached to Mr French.

Anh appeared at the glass partition door.

"Where you go this morning?"

Venglish had become Lillian's mother tongue.

"I go to market, then I go my sister's, then I go shopping. Look, I buy you this."

Anh beamed as she handed Lillian the white diamante watch in her hand.

"You are such a sweetheart. Do you know that? You cheered me right up."

Anh smiled like a proud child as Lillian pretended to like it.

"You welcome. Hey, we go to Tanh Hoa again on Monday?"

"Yes. We'll be spending most of our mornings in the medical centre in Tanh Hoa city, OK? And in the evening we'll travel into the country."

"No ploblem. Dat fine. Tonight we go to Dragonfly?"

"Where?"

"Oh, it pub. It good fun. We can have shisha pipe."

"How about the French cinema instead?"

"Why you so boring? You not have drink yet in Hanoi. Come on. You must come."

"Am…well, OK."

Why am I hiding my pregnancy from her?

The thought tumbled around her brain.

Because Phil needs to be the first to know.

Thank you, Controller; my voice of reason, my backbone.

33.

The arresting beauty of rural Vietnam wasn't enough to still Lillian's whirl-wind. As she looked upon spiky green jungles fringing the boundaries of paddy fields, she sighed, aware of and guilty about her lack of gratitude for magnificence. Karst limestone mountains stood high over dirt roads cleaving through lush, exotic flora. A mellow red river meandered under old cargo bridges, heavy with the sediments it had been accumulating since China.

I'm pregnant, I'm fat, my boyfriend doesn't know a thing—and I'm about to go, I can't say this, undercover? On a highly dangerous operation? Who am I?

A catapulting thump on the breaks forced her attention outward. It was the adrenaline-junkie driver. Again. He fearlessly ploughed bent-axle-first into gaping hazards and pot holes, lapping up the force of his rattles by curling his tongue into the corner of his mouth.

Weirdo.

Lillian channelled her anger into psychoanalysis.

A typical case of small man syndrome. A tiny Asian male like him has to make an impact somehow. He gets his kicks on the roads, and grins—actually grins—when putting lives in danger. It makes him feel in-control—powerful, even. Asshole!

His fetish for all things undulating and flinty was testing Lillian who, along with Anh and the medical staff, was being flicked like a pawn about the back. Lillian moved her eyes round and searched for someone to share her frustration. No one batted a raven eyelash.

Accept what you can't control.

Fine. But how?

Distract yourself.

Buffalos ploughing fields. Barefooted women and children bending over to plant seeds.

Nice.

Phil cradling our baby.

Gorgeous!

Decorating the nursery.

Heaven!

Baptsim.

Will we?

First steps.

Awwww.

"LEELEEANNE, we go macket now. Come on! We got fiteen minutes."

Monster Man parked in the twilight zone; to where some zombie sixth sense had led a crowd of traders. Nothing: no village, hamlet, parish or settlement surrounded the isolated trading hub for hundreds of miles. Inside a fenced field, flimsy corrugated roofs leaned on white stone pillars, creating a framework for trading stalls. Merchants arranged products with limitless creativity. One woman had placed the entire insides of a pig in anatomical order—the heart at the centre, the intestines below…. She squatted above the massacred animal holding a butcher's knife and smiled with innocent eyes.

Only in Vietnam.

People stared at Lillian.

"Anh, have these people ever seen a white person?"

"Probally not. They not go to Hanoi; it too far. And Tanh Hoa not in Lonely Planet. Maybe for some, it first time they see white person."

Women smiled as wide as their jaw muscles would flex, parading brown teeth. The braver ones reached out to touch Lillian as though she were a wishing stone.

"Anh, let's go. We need to get to the clinic before lunch."

"But..."

"But no."

"Figh. If you say so."

"I say so."

Women from the region's Hmong ethnic group heard about Care about Children's day clinic through Lillian's local poster-campaign blitz.

Eat your heart out, Marianne, she mwuh-ha-d, watching the province's poorest children arrive with their mothers in droves.

The makeshift surgery was just outside the city, beside a bus stop, and was borderline hygienic. Lillian commanded the chief of her medical staff to round up his workforce for her introductory speech. Anh translated in a way that made everyone feel at ease. The only thing marring the atmosphere was the pitiful sight of People Committee Officials in the corner.

With a care system in place, Anh, Lillian, Nurse and Monster Man filed into the white Toyota van for the village rounds, arriving at a tiny settlement after an hour on the road.

A steaming stall offering *pho*—what Lillian now understood was Vietnam's prized soupy noodle dish—stood outside the local undertakers. Wooden coffins spilled out onto the dirt road in sight of passers by; a smattering of tall and skinny brick houses cheering up the macabre centrepiece. The foursome walked towards the only building showing life and enquired about the local population. The only man inside pointed them to a village in the mountains where, he said, the tribe people lived.

The driver started up the van and drove the dirt roads until he found a group of people clustered at the centre of a neighbourhood of stilt houses. The entire community was dressed in every print, stripe, fabric and colour of traditional ethnic garb.

Wow, this is amazing, Lillian gasped.

Children ran around the van in circles, jumping and screaming.

Anh opened the van door and introduced Lillian to the flabbergasted hermetic community who spoke little Vietnamese.

Lillian stood over the group and asked Anh to translate her words. When the public address finished, a woman attached herself to Anh's ear while staring at Lillian.

"You want to stay here tonigh? This woman want us stay. It roo say no."

"Everything's rude to you, Anh."

"No it not."

'OK. What exactly does she want?'

"She want to cook dinner and for you spend nigh."

Lillian looked around at the stunning scenery and realised it was an opportunity not to be missed.

132

"Tell her I would be delighted."

"Yes?"

"Yes. We can leave early in the morning."

As Anh conveyed Lillian's response, the woman screeched into laughter, covering her mouth with her hands, like a child hearing something too good to be true. Lillian saw the best of humankind pour through the humble woman before her, who, she thought, hadn't been spoiled by the ego westerners prized.

I'm changing. Vietnam is changing me.

Lillian made her way with Anh to the woman's stilt house.

It stood tall over a patchwork of rice fields, offering the perfect vantage point for the expected full moon. To the Vietnamese, Anh explained to Lillian, the night of a full moon was the most auspicious in the lunar calendar. In quiet anticipation, the crowd waited for it, taking in the evening's orange sun as it melted into the horizon.

When the dark of night arrived, dangling rainbow lanterns lit up the boundaries of rice fields. Each glittering hue fused expertly with the glow of the full moon, as though designed. Beauty reigned supreme; captivating; seducing Lillian, who was floating now—over cultural divides, language, custom and every other unnatural concept mankind used to divide existence from truth. She glimpsed freedom.

This is like nothing I have ever known. Vietnam is changing me.

"Come, come now."

Anh gently waved Lillian inside the house.

A teenage girl with warm eyes sat down beside Lillian. There was no hint, she thought, of a hormonal 'troubled teenager' in her. Maybe psychological labels put on dysfunction are nothing more than that, Lillian thought, folding a blanket into a seat. Carefree, she let her mind dissolve in the romance of the velvet night. A waterfall of peace crashed over her analytical mind, sending out ripple-waves of perfect peace to everyone in the room.

Vietnam is changing me.

Baskets of malleable sticky rice passed round in baskets, with a side of crushed nuts. A quiet man whom she hadn't yet heard speak gently rolled a portion of rice into a cylinder with his bare hands. He handed it to her and bowed his head. She replicated the act of humility.

Older men and women, inspired by the charged environment, unleashed their party tricks: stories, poems, songs, musical performances and even, to Lillian's enchantment, water puppets in the rice fields. There was a baffling paradox at the very core of these people, she thought, looking around at their childlike playfulness. They were tough enough to defeat brutal enemies and yet, at the same time, were openly vulnerable. Did it really happen; Lillian asked herself, that B52s dropped bombs onto serene villages like this? Where people just wanted to sit in circles? Lillian took a moment to scold the ghosts of politicians past. Humankind wasn't all kind, but here, now, in this moment, it was everything she had ever hoped it to be.

Vietnam has changed me.

34.

Lillian woke to the sound of a cock crowing, her first time to experience waking to world's most universal alarm, clichéd and all as it was. She laughed about it, since she was from rural Ireland. Her mother had an odd phobia that rationalised screaming in horror on sight of anything from the poultry variety.

Good old Nuala, Lillian thought, smiling.

The smell of last night's turf fire moved through the air. Quietly, she tiptoed over the bodies around her and unzipped the mosquito net.

Silence ruled, allowing only the sound of tired, sleeping breaths into its gilded empire. There was no peace like the early morning; she was beginning to see with her new perspective. The rest of the day seemed to spin chaotically, too busy manifesting human thoughts and desires to bask in its own stillness.

Yes. The day is still. It's us that make it chaotic.

Nature's ticklish breeze, sparkling dew and falling petals needed nothing but itself, she could now see.

I wish I could be like that.

The selfish wish pushed past her nature-inspired contentment, releasing the first poison of the day into the ether.

Don't be so harsh on yourself. Who doesn't want more? If you didn't want more you'd be dead.

The Controller usurped the driving reigns. It was time for dawn to become day, with all its chores and responsibilities and practicalities.

Magic is for daydreamers, not the ambitious.

"Em oi, it's morning! Wake up sleepy head. And wake the nurse and the driver."

35.

"Phil, please don't be like this.'

She was doing it again, he thought—pushing his feelings away. She had no idea how selfish she was for someone who called herself a do-gooder.

"Lillian, I wasn't going to say this because you had a lot on before you left, but I'm saying it now."

"OK. Say it."

"You forgot our anniversary, Lillian. It was the night of your going away party. I had a plan for us. But you...you left me in a corner with a flirting couple and ignored me the whole night."

Jesus Christ. That was why. That was the reason for your crappy behaviour.

Her heart sunk to her boots.

"I don't know what to say. I'm mortified. I'm ashamed. I'm so sorry. I just had so much on."

Like being pregnant with your child.

"So much on that you forgot about us?"

"Guilty."

"I have to go, Lillian. I've been waiting for your call all afternoon."

That's mature.

"I told you it'd take time to get back to Hanoi and that I might be a bit late."

"A bit, Lillian. You told me you'd be a bit late. Three hours isn't a bit late—it's a lot late."

"Phil, I'm sorry. I really am."

"I'll speak to you tomorrow."

No, you won't actually. Because I'm going undercover.

"Bye, Phil…I love you."

"Ya, you too."

It wasn't I love you, she realised, but it was—at the very least—a response. She closed her laptop and sat rigid on the soft beanbag.

What am I doing?

Gerard was showering in the bathroom.

Why did I invite him to spend the night?

It's easy and straightforward, that's why. Dam Trau is closer to the airport than where he lives. There's nothing to figure out.

The Controller was back, steady and reliable.

"Lillian, would you like to watch this old movie with me tonight?"

Is he really standing in front of me in just a towel? What the fuck is he at?

She scolded herself for allowing him to think she was single.

An old movie!

138

How textbook is that?!

But he does look handsome, with his sun kissed muscles and unshaved roughness.

Stop entertaining those thoughts.

Cop on to yourself.

"Am...sure, why not?"

Who is this person talking?

36.

Gerard was being moody. *What an ass*, Lillian thought, sitting up in her seat. She had been unable to tactfully ignore the last of his awkward passes the night before, and ended up telling him—in unambiguous terms—to back off. He had been whimpering since.

"What's the plan when we get to Ho Chi Minh?"

Gerard didn't look up from his German magazine.

"Are you going to spend the entire flight ignoring me?"

She raised an eyebrow flirtatiously, willing him to see through his childish behaviour.

"No, I'm just really quite tired. That mattress was not so comfortable."

At last, a little warm.

"But yes, Lillian, when we get there we will meet the camera crew, a local translator and, of course, my source. He hasn't given me any details yet. We will simply go where he tells us to go and then, at a certain point, he will leave. He does not want to be seen in the village."

Lillian's inner body vibrated with suspense.

"So, how *did* you find your source, Gerard?"

She spoke with a gentleness she was sure would win him round.

"If I told you, I would have to kill you."

He laughed as though it were an original joke.

"Curiosity killed the cat but—remember—a cat has nine lives."

He erupted into laughter.

Geek, Lillian thought, smiling.

"You are a very strange girl. Are you aware of this fact?"

"Yes, I am. Now tell me."

Geek.

He stirred a little in his seat and pulled on his jeans to free some space around his crotch.
Ick.

"My source used to be a member of the criminal gang we are today exposing. He turned a leaf, so to speak, and moved to Hanoi."

He looked at Lillian with eyes that asked if she was following. It was odd that he did that so much, she thought, since he spent so much time praising her for her 'in-depth knowledge of global social issues.'

"Yes, I get it. Go on..."

"He became a friend of Duc. You remember that arty pub where we met? It was called Duc's?"

"Yes..."

"Well, Duc owns it."

No way.

"He likes to invite progressive thinkers to meet there and share ideas and thoughts. He feels that the system is wrong in Vietnam and that Vietnamese people should unite to tear down the veil of secrecy and censorship in the country, so to speak. You know?"

"Uhm hmm..."

"So, being the man he is, Duc took this ex-criminal under his wing. Duc approached me a few months later and asked me how I would feel about telling the truth about these guys, you know?"

"Wow! You were very lucky to land such a scoop."

"Yes, I was very lucky. But it is also very fortunate for an NGO officer to get the chance to tag along. Is this not so, Lillian?"

"I feel *very* lucky."

37.

Lillian's nerves formed an iron chain of fear around her organs. She convinced herself that the faintness she was feeling wasn't fear, just her survival instincts kicking in; just science. She tried again to hide her physical symptoms. If Gerard copped it, he'd send her back to the hotel.

Oh holy fuck, oh holy fuck. What am I doing? What am I doing?

Gerard briefed his camera crew in German. Lillian's thoughts kicked inside her head.

It'll all be over in a few hours.

She stood at the edge of the group; arms folded, and diverted her attention to her right foot, which was forming circles in the dirt road.

"Lillian, come here please."

Gerard's tone was uncharacteristically authoratative.

"Lillian, you understand that you are to do nothing, yes?"

"Yes. I understand. I will do nothing. I will wait in the van."

"It is important for your safety that you do. Is this clear?"

How many times is he going to ask?

"Yes. It. Is. Clear."

"Fine. Get in the van please."

She took a seat in the back. Gerard's source sat in the front and spoke to the translator, who then addressed the group. Everyone was dressed casually, except for the source, who was wearing a baseball cap, an oversized jacket and sun glasses. His fear of being conspicuous had made him just that.

Idiot.

Fear casts people out of the excellence zone. . .fear casts people out of the excellence zone. . . fear casts people out of the excellence zone.

She repeated it over and over.

Fear is more dangerous than danger itself. I mean, look at that fool in the front.

"We will be driving close to the Cambodian border. Once there, my source, who I will call Long, will leave us. He cannot be seen in Chau Doc. The risk is too great that someone might see him. We will be on our own from there until we reach Tinh Bien. Is everyone OK with this?"

Lillian's mouth opened of its own volition.

"Yes."

The driver turned the key in the van and resumed his private war against shoddy roads. No one spoke. Occasional smooth roads did little to tranquilise the nervous atmosphere. Only the sporadic sounds of throats clearing or phones beeping broke the quiet.

"We are here. Long is now leaving us."

Long got out of the van at the edge of Chau Doc, the last town before Tinh Bien, and stretched the peak of his cap over his face. He zipped his jacket to the neck and walked away in a hurry. He looked silly. If Lillian hadn't been so petrified, she thought, she would have laughed.

The gang would be arriving in Tinh Bien within the hour, Long informed Gerard. The driver restarted the engine and headed towards it, parking the van within walking distance of its local *bia hoi,* or beer house.

The village was patrolled by border control units. Only a few miles away, officials manned posts with guns and rubber stamps.

How in God's name could a criminal gang possibly get children across without getting caught?

"Gerard, can you please tell me how the hell they get children across this border? They're manned by officials."

Gerard looked shocked.

"Are you really asking me this?"

Lillian felt embarrassed for not understanding why her question was stupid.

"The officials can be *bought,* Lillian. They make a lot of money from trafficking. This is arguably the worst part of the whole sordid thing."

FUCK. Now he thinks I'm stupid.

Gerard went over the plan to the group.

"Before they bring the children across the border, a gang of four men will hand them over to two other men who will be waiting here—at this bia hoi—to pick them up. It has worked this way for months."

He met everyone's eye and continued.

"The only action anyone will take is our translator, who will attempt to speak to the gang and get them to open up. If and when they do, he will fake an interest in their business, asking where they have come from and where they are going. That is it. He will be wearing a hidden camera. This is all we need for this documentary to be successful."

The cameramen ran through the technological functions of the camera with the translator for the seventeenth time.

"Stop this. He knows how it works. Do you want to be seen?"

Gerard was agitated. The tech guys stopped what they were doing.

"Let's go. Lillian, you can come with us. You will sit in the *bia hoi* with me and the boys. Our translator will arrive after us and sit on his own. We will watch him from a distance. Is that clear?"

Lillian gulped powdered saliva.

"Yes. I'm fine with that."

"Good, now bring your lonely planet and camera. It is important we look like tourists."

"Sure. That's a good idea."

"And finally, just be calm. Are you calm?"

As the Dalai Lama. I'm about to puke, idiot.

"Totally, yes...I'm perfect."

"OK then, let's go. Ladies first."

"OK then."

Lillian sat in the bia hoi looking for ways to divert her fear-fixed attention. She soon found a subject for a psychoanalysis lesson: a young girl with dripping-wet dark hair down to her hips. Lillian spotted a basin of soapy water by the entrance of the *bia hoi*. Two used sachets of shampoo were strewn beside it, the same one she had been using herself since her first night in the hotel.

Maybe there's only one type of shampoo in the country.

Vietnam is a businessman's dream.

The girl wasn't more than sixteen, Lillian guessed, and was dutifully serving beer to men who didn't look at her. Unbothered, she approached Lillian's table. Gerard addressed her in Vietnamese and she smiled back, revealing brown teeth. She nodded her small head shyly as a way to tell him she had no idea what he was saying.

Gerard looked at Lillian.

"I am really quite annoyed. I told her in her own language that I wanted four beers."

Lillian pointed to the bottles of Tiger beer in the fridge and held up four fingers. Words weren't always necessary, either was anger.

Christ, what a dumbass. He'll blow his own cover.

Bia Hoi's were funny things, she thought, and the same everywhere: basically roofed structures on a series of pillars. It was a funny sight, in her opinion, to see grown men sitting on teeny plastic furniture while acting macho. Each man's facial expression was aggressive, serious.

As if they get to do serious with their small asses sitting on kid's furniture.

"The translator has just come in. Don't look over, please."

"Does this translator have a name?" Lillian asked Gerard, calmed a little by the beer.

Gerard laughed in relief.

"Of course. I should really have introduced him by his name. It's Tam."

"Well I'll be sure to say hello to him properly once this is all over."

Gerard smiled at her, impressed again by her cool demeanour.

"Take out your guidebook, please, and open it up on Ho Chi Minh City."

Lillian picked up her backpack and poked around, pulling out her torch and first aid kit on her way to the bottom.

"Aha, found it."

"Good. Now open it and study the streets around the airport, OK?"

"OK."

Why is he asking me this?

She tried to concentrate but her peripheral attention glued itself to the gang members who had just walked in. She watched on as they ordered the children to sit on the low wall outside.

Gerard called Tam's phone from his pocket.

Tam got up from his chair in the corner and stood next to the children outside with his phone to his ear.

He hung up, lit a cigarette, and engaged the children in conversation.

The men inside stared out, noticeably alarmed.

Lillian's mouth dried up.

She sucked on the neck of the beer bottle.

The men looked away.

Phew

Minutes passed as hours as Tam chatted 'casually' with the gang members.

Her eyes stopped on a boy; a helpless, distressed and terrified boy dressed in a tattered red vest. He sobbed alone outside the *bia hoi* with his hands pressed to his face. Desperate to keep his crying quiet, he forced the bulging veins in his neck to take the pressure as he silenced his grief. No one comforted him.

A gang member stood up and taunted him with a cruel impression. His ridicule turned the boy hysterical. The gang leader responded by stampeding towards him and slapping him over the head. The girl with the long, wet hair sat with her back turned and arms folded. Male laughter filled the space in the *bia hoi*, including Tam's, whose acting skills were beginning to repulse Lillian.

Stupid, stupid, stupid Bastards.

"Lillian, the streets—I need you to familiarise yourself with the streets. Got it?"

Fuck you, Gerard.

"Fine. Alright."

Tam left the *bia hoi* and turned for the border. Two men followed and walked towards parked scooters with the children. The boy in the red vest pleaded with the men and dragged his heels.

"Hey, YOU—he doesn't want to go. Stop hitting him."

Gerard pulled on Lillian's t-shirt.

"LILLIAN! WHAT ARE YOU'RE DOING?"

"Shut up, Gerard, you PUSSY. How could you just stand there and do *nothing*? How can you call yourself a *man*? All you give a shit about is your documentary, your *ego*."

She slapped his hand and freed herself.

"Yes, you, I'm talking to you. What do you think you're doing?"

One of the men reacted by reaching into his pocket.

"What? Are you going to take out a weapon? It's not smart to kill an Irish citizen in Vietnam, you *moron*. Unless you want to get caught? Your balls aren't so big now, are they?"

He looked at his accomplice to verify the white girl in front of him was for real. He walked to Lillian and breathed his cigarette smoke into her face.

Gerard pulled at her.

"LILLIAN! YOU ARE PUTTING OUR LIVES IN DANGER. STOP THIS."

His voice turned to a piercing ring. Brambly bushes knotted around her throat, choking her. A '96 red Ford Orion ploughed through puddles of blood.

The boy in the tattered red vest was gone. Stephen was gone.

Gone.

Gone.

Gone.

She spun down a vortex of grief into nothingness.

A violent shake pulled her back. Gerard's face appeared through haze.

"YOU BITCH! You promised not to do *anything*. These guys will be hunted down and caught after this documentary is aired—*I* plan to make sure of that. Tam is gone to the border to film officials taking bribes right now. How *dare* you put all of our lives in danger. My crew have *families* Lillian—children and wives to go home to. You had *no* right."

The driver drove at full speed.

"I'm sorry, Stephen. I'm so sorry, Stephen. Forgive me, Stephen. Forgive me."

"Who the fuck is Stephen? Shut up."

38.

"Is there anyone home to look after you?"

The driver pulled up at the edge of the busy road near the entrance of Dam Trau.

"Anh should be home."

Gerard threw out her backpack and slid the door shut.

Without thoughts, Lillian made her way to A8.

'Lee-lee-anne! I miss you!'

Anh's cheer assaulted her.

"Lee-lee-anne? You hear me? I say I miss you!"

Lillian dropped her bag on the floor and curled up on her mattress.

"What matter? You sick?"

"Go away and leave me alone."

39.

"Richard, she was supposed to call this morning. I mean, she's seven hours ahead. It's not like she doesn't have the whole day to plan the phonecall."

She has a point. Lillian is slacking.

"I'll give her till noon. We'll start worrying then."

"Fine, Richard, but please don't say you weren't warned when she tells us she's gone and cocked it up for us."

"Always the harbinger of doom, aren't you Marianne?"

That was uncalled for, she thought. She was a professional. Just because her predictions were negative, did not mean they were not accurate.

"Richard, I don't sugar-coat, you know that about me."

"I do, I really do."

40.

"I'm sick and tired of her bullshit. She only cares about herself."

Guy didn't know how to respond.

"Maybe she's just stuck in the back arse of nowhere, mate. Maybe she just can't get to a phone."

"Phones work there, Guy. Vietnam's a developing country, but it has almost FULL network coverage. She can't use that one."

His behaviour was bordering on obsessive.

"How about another beea, mate? Might loosen ya up a bit!"

"It's Monday and I'm in court tomorrow with the biggest case of my career and she doesn't even know. What am I supposed to do, Guy? Should I be putting up with this shit?"

Guy tried to avert Phil's serial killer eyes.

"I don't know, mate. Just wait until she calls before making any rash decisions."

41.

It was 6 pm and time to go home.

"You see, Richard, I knew it. I knew we should have hired more *experienced* project managers."

Couldn't she just shut it.

"We'll speak about this in the morning, Marianne."

Richard sat at his desk.

What if she's in trouble with the law?

What if she's messed the operation up?

Enough of the what ifs, Richard. Pull yourself together, Man.

42.

"Pat, I can't believe she hasn't called us yet. She promised me she'd call the weekend. It's Tuesday."

"Ah now, Nuala, don't be making a fuss over nothing."

Did he not care about his own flesh and blood? Their daughter was in Vietnam—*alone*. Any oul weirdo could have attacked her and left her in a rainforest somewhere.

"I'm calling her boss in London. Richard, I think his name is Richard. I have to. She's left me no choice.'"

"I think you're overreacting."

"And I think you don't care."

"I do so."

"Well prove it then. Get my address book out of the dresser drawer."

43.

Thursday and still not a word.

"Richard, I'm really very worried now. Do we have to send someone out there? I mean, we can't very well call the Vietnamese Embassy and tell them that our representative has gone AWOL?"

"That's exactly what we have to do."

"But won't that risk our entire project?"

"Yes, maybe, but she could be in danger. She really could. And frankly, I'm worried sick about her."

Marianne thought seriously about what he had just said. She wouldn't have called Lillian a friend, but Christ, she wouldn't wish any harm to come to her.

"Do you think someone might have hurt her? I have the number for her translator. Can't we try her first? I don't know why I didn't think of her sooner."

"Call her now, Marianne. You really could have suggested this earlier."

44.

L illian was being crucified by an inner parasite. It had taken form as a hell-ish current of quivering energy, spinning furiously through her twisted insides. It was tearing her apart; gnawing on her last nerves; stealing her breath. She sobbed desperately, hopelessly begging God to intervene. There was nothing she could do to fight it. It had taken over.

Sweat flowed from her brow. Her breath wasn't her own, but as if by some sick physical law, her attention was permanently forced on its shallow, rapid movements. She was terrorised.

"Lee-lee-anne. You need wake up. I worried now. Your boss call me. He worried too. So your mam…and I worried, too. You cry a lot. Please, I call my sister if you don't talk to me."

"I'll call them. I'll call my boss."

Lillian sat up.

"Anh, help me."

Anh looked at her friend and felt her fear. What was happening to her?

45.

"Richard, you'll need to sit down for this one."

"What is it, tell me."

'I spoke to her translator. Lillian is physically fine.'

"Oh thank God. Phew. What a relief. You wouldn't believe the nightmares I had thought up."

"But she's not fine *mentally*, if you know what I mean."

Marianne was making a strange gesture with her mouth, as though what she was about to say were disgraceful.

"No, I don't know. What *do* you mean?"

"From what her translator said—who by the way doesn't have very good English—she's had a bit of a breakdown. She's been in bed for four days."

"Pardon me?"

"I know. I don't know the circumstances. She was in Ho Chi Minh City over the weekend and when she got back she was 'strange', according to her translator."

"Strange?"

"Yes, strange."

"What the bloody hell was she doing in Ho Chi Minh City?"

"I don't know, Richard."

"We need to call her mother. She's worried about her...I'm not sure this news will put her at ease."

Richard darted to the ringing phone.

"Hello, Richard speaking."

"LILLIAN!"

Marianne rushed to his side, ears cocked.

"What's she saying?"

"Shhh, Marianne."

Lillian could hear her in the background. She'd be delighted with all of this, she thought.

"It's OK, Lillian. Take your time. Just speak."

Marianne clenched fists were preventing an outburst. She paced the floor.

"Why didn't you tell us? I have to say it: I'm disappointed."

Disappointed? Why? What has that Irish nutter gone and done now? This is going to be juicy.

Marianne's imagination speculated furiously.

"Lillian, you're off the project. Pack your things, you're coming home. I'm talking tomorrow, Lillian."

SHE'S OFF THE PROJECT?!

Marianne stopped herself from opening the door and shouting the scandalous news.

"Don't worry about that. I'll get in touch with the People's Committee. We'll send someone in your place. It'll be fine. Just get back here safe."

He put the phone down and breathed a long sigh into his hands.

"Richard, what's happened?"

There was no way he was going to give the ice queen ammunition to tear Lillian apart further.

"Get back to work, Marianne. I'll brief the rest of the team tomorrow. Get Sarah Murphy into my office. Go."

46.

"Thank you for calling, Richard. I appreciate it."

Nuala put down the receiver and cursed the heavens. Hadn't she suffered enough already?

"Pat, she's not well; Lillian—she has to come home. She's had, a...I don't know. I think, a...one of those...breakdowns."

"One of those *what?*"

"She was at the Cambodian border saving a child or something. She hasn't moved from the bed in days. Her boss has sent her home."

"Wouldn't she try to save herself instead of always being out trying to save the world? She'd want to stop that fooling around now and get out of her bed. She needs to hold on to that good job."

"You don't understand, Pat. She might not be right again."

"Ah, stop that foolish talk Nuala, one head case is enough in the family."

"God forgive you for saying that, Pat. She's our daughter, our *only* daughter."

Nuala slammed the kitchen door closed and ran out to the garden.

She sat down beside a cluster of hyacinths and chrysanthemums, close to Stephen's tree. She put her hand to her chest, feeling fresh pain ooze through an old wound.

Where am I going to find the strength?

47.

"Mind yourself, Mrs O'Shea. I'll take care of her. "

Phil put the phone down and groaned.

Debbie walked out of Ray's office.

"Hey, Philly—lighten up. May never happen! Are you coming for drinks? Ray is right chuffed with you. I bet he makes you partner soon."

Debbie hadn't done so bad either. They had used the precedent she had researched as the backbone of their case.

"I don't know, Debs. I've just got some bad news."

"It's not Lillian, is it?"

"It is. She's safe but she's not well. She's coming home tomorrow night."

"Oh. Shall I leave you alone then?"

"Maybe I should be alone, but I'd prefer to get quite *pissed*, actually."

"Then come on, let's go! I'll make you all better!"

48.

Nothing around her had the power to shift her attention from what was going on inside. A part of her was burning up; her guts were roasting on a spit, churning sluggishly around her nerves. She was dying a slow and painful death. The background static of high anxiety was interrupted in hourly intervals by flash floods of terror. The panic defibrillated her chest, forcing her to tremble and quake. It was taking her to the brink of insanity. Every time she fought it, it tightened its grip.

"You bag checked in, Lee-lee-ann."

Lillian could barely hear Anh over the noise of horrifying mental movies. A mean voice in her head had started to berate her, telling her she had screwed everything up, that she was guilty, that she was weak.

"Take these tablets, I get them from my sister. They make you sleep. I leave my Skype username in your bag. Call me."

Lillian uttered inaudible words and wrapped her arms around Anh. After a few long minutes, Anh undid herself and wiped teardrops from Lillian's cheeks.

"It OK, you be fine. I sad like this when my mam and brother die, too. It OK. You will be strong again."

Lillian turned and walked through the departure doors. She opened the cap of her water bottle and swigged enough to swallow four maximum-dose sedatives.

49.

"I need you to relocate to Hanoi. I'm talking within the next few days."

Sarah closed her mouth to stop her jaw hitting the floor.

"The next few *days*? Will I be working with Lillian?"

Richard considered his words.

"No, you won't. Because Lillian got herself into trouble and left me with no choice. I kicked her off the project."

Sarah was dumbfounded.

"You kicked her off the project?! Why? What happened?"

"I'll let you in on all of that after you give me your answer. Yes or no, Sarah. I'm sorry to put you into this position but you're my next best development officer and I'm in a pretty serious bind. The Vietnamese authorities are already getting paranoid."

She didn't know what to say. Would she be crossing her friend if she said yes? No. She had to consider herself first; it was *her* career, after all.

"Yes, I'll do it. I can do it. I took Lillian's classes so I have an idea. And...I've been researching for out first report. I've been to Vietnam, too. I can do this, Richard."

"I'll remember this. Thank you."

50.

"Are you OK, darling? Why didn't you call? Your father and I were beside ourselves."

Lillian didn't believe that her father was 'beside himself' with anything.

"Seoul, where's that? Will you be coming home to Ireland for a while?"

Pat didn't look up from *The Irish Times,* but stopped reading. He did care.

"I don't *believe* it! She's not coming home. She's staying in London. She won't even come home for a break. I'm so cross with her."

"She'll be fine. She always is."

That was enough. She was sick and tired of listening to his careless assurances.

"Pat, are you ever going to come to life again? Look at you, sitting in your chair—dead to the world and dead to your family. Have you *anything* left inside you heart?"

And off she went crying again. She was doing that a lot lately. It wasn't his way. He didn't have to prove himself to anybody. Didn't he work hard all his life to provide for Lillian? No one had the right to tell him he didn't care.

51.

It was getting harder to hold on. Nothing meant anything. What was the point? People didn't care. It was all about greed and corruption and competition and *money*. She had done everything she could to go the other way; to help the world change, but she couldn't do it alone anymore. The boy in the red vest haunted her. Stephen haunted her.

Why go on?

She would always end up back at the same place; back to disappointment and hurt and failure. Maybe she should have listened to her detractors. Maybe she should forget about being able to make the world and its children happy.

She emptied the contents of her makeup bag in the ceramic sink at Heathrow Airport. It had been an agonising flight. The sedatives had worn off by Korea, forcing her to come down in misery. Her throat quivered as she thought of Phil waiting in arrivals. It wasn't fair to him to have to see her like this. He deserved better. He was going to be the perfect father. Her life, she decided, was about the baby now. Too long she had thought only of herself.

She wheeled her luggage through to arrivals and searched the terminal for Phil and flowers. Five minutes passed.

Twenty.

An hour.

Phil's never late.

She took a seat, surrendering to the fact that he wasn't coming. Had she emailed him her flight number? It was likely her mistake, she figured, walking towards a cab.

She tip toed through the apartment door and threw her bags in the corner. The air was fusty, as though light hadn't entered in weeks. Someone had used her potpourri as an ashtray. She recognised the red wine bottles on the coffee table as the present Phil's father had given them last Christmas. They were both empty, beside two emptier glasses. Her heart thumped. She walked to the bedroom. There was no way her suspicions would add up to the truth.

She stood frozen.

"LILLIAN!"

A surge of shock ripped her up.

"TANYA!' You cheat on me with a woman who made a moron out of you? You PUSSY! Why are all men such PUSSIES!"

In the pit of her stomach, waves of bile churned round and round, aggravating her guts. She paused at the door and tried to catch her breath.

"Lillian, I was going to tell you…"

Phil was standing in a towel, grabbing her arm.

"Fuck you. Don't talk to me, don't touch me, *don't* LOOK at me."

"Lillian, *you* dumped *me*, you know. You haven't loved me for a long time. You brought this on yourself."

Was she hearing things? There was nothing she could say to such cruel, twisted, sordid thinking.

"You set me up, you prick. You wanted revenge for the time *I* dumped *you*. I was confused. I loved you, Phil. I was confused. I was about to give you everything."

He was disgusted with himself.

"Don't fucking cry into my face, you piece of shit."

He grabbed her as she opened the door.

"I said don't touch me, you lowlife."

She ran down the stairs, through the exit to the curb outside and rocked back and forth.

What's happening? What's happening? It's too much, it's too much.

Her body shook. She took her phone out of her handbag, dropped it on the road, picked it up, and dropped it again.

Oh God, Oh God, Oh God.

52.

"What are you going to do about Lillian?"

Marianne was desperate for Richard to make a decision. She had broken protocol, jeopardised the entire project and failed to contact them for four days. Surely, he was going to give her more than just a slap on the wrist.

"I don't know."

He liked Lillian. She was an outstanding development officer. But she had made a mess of things. What kind of an example would he be setting if he didn't at least punish her?

"Well, she'll be here tomorrow. You need to decide."

"I'm aware of that, Marianne."

"Well, then?"

"I said I don't know. Maybe I'll suspend her."

"*Suspend* her. Is that it, Richard? Maybe I'll just disappear for a week then. And will you be paying her for this 'suspension?"

"I hadn't thought about it."

"Dear god she's got you in her grips. So you're giving her a holiday?"

"No, Marianne. It's likely I won't be paying her. We'll wait until she comes in tomorrow and see what she has to say for herself."

He was such a softy. She was losing respect for him. He knew it.

53.

"Lillian, please take a breath. Please talk to me."

Nuala held her hand over the receiver to mute the sound of her own tears.

"It's OK, love. Just let it out. Tell me what happened."

"Phil?"

"He never..."

"Come home, please come home."

She hung up the phone and threw a porcelain ornament against the tiled floor. Pat could see where his daughter got her sense of drama.

"This is worse than the movies. How much trauma is one person supposed to take in the space of twenty four *bloody* hours? Oh, Pat, what's happening to her?"

"Whist up and tell me."

"That fella of hers that we called a fine young man is no better than a criminal. She's after walking in on him with another woman. At a time like this. Can you believe it?"

It wasn't the most tragic fate that could befall a person, Pat coolly reasoned. Why his wife and daughter continued to delude themselves about the source of their unhappiness escaped him. But—and he was guilty of it himself—it was easier to misdirect uncomfortable emotions than deal with raw ones dead on. As a family, they had grown accustomed to ignoring pink elephants.

"Is she coming home?"

"She's back at work tomorrow."

"Maybe we could go over to her?"

Nula threw her arms around her husband.

54.

"Well done, chicken. I'm happy for you! But what the bloody 'eck is after happening to our Lillian?"

"It seems she's had a bit of a…a kind of a…breakdown?"

It was hard for Sarh get her lips around the taboo.

"Oh," Scott replied.

"I *know*. I don't know how to react either."

"Maybe we should just say nothing."

"Suppose."

"But you! Get you, you big Superstar! You've passed me *right* out!"

"I passed you out years ago!"

Lillian was already yesterday's news.

55.

Jessie had to get rid of Guy before Lillian arrived.

"Why do I have to go just because she's coming?"

He was being petulant again.

"Because I said so. She's my fried and your friend has just fucked her over. I'm sure she doesn't want to see you. Now get up and go."

"Fine, but I'm having a shower first."

He's such a baby, she thought.

"*Hurry* on."

There was a knock at the door.

"Lillian, sweetheart, are you OK?"

The husk of a girl in front of her looked worse than she thought she would.

"Jessie, I don't know what's happening to me..."

Jessie reached her arms around her to prevent her spotting the empty beer cans.

"Were you guys out last night, too?"

"I wasn't, Guy was."

"Oh yeah, with Phil?"

"Yeah, I think so."

"Was *Tanya* out with them too?"

"Am...I think so. But I wasn't there last night, Lillian. You believe me on that, don't you?"

"Had you met her out before?"

Loaded question, Jessie thought.

"Am...yeah...but I never spoke to her. She was just in the same...circle."

Lillian said nothing, just slouched back onto the couch.

Guy came out of the bedroom and searched around for his keys.

"Hi, Lillian. Welcome home."

"Fuck you, Guy, you back-stabber."

Was he hearing things?

"Pardon me?"

"I said: fuck you, you back-stabber."

"What are you talking about, Lillian? All I did was spend hours listening to *your* boyfriend moan and whine about how his girlfriend ditched *him*. Don't feel sorry for yourself now. You were the one who ignored him while you were away.'

His reasoning was the same as Phil's. The pair of bastards.

"You're a scum bag."

"Hey, Lillian, get a grip. That's my boyfriend you're talking to."

"Run for your life, Ruth. He's a cheap slut, too. It's a club."

"Lillian, get out. You're totally out of line. Go. Leave."
"I'd be happy to."
Another bridge burned.

56.

There was nowhere to hide. It had moved into every cell of her body. The pain was worse, she imagined, than a terminal illness. She cried and cried and cried.

Rejection, rejection, rejection. Say it, Lillian—re-jec-tion. Why do you think you always get REJECTED? Might there be a pattern here? Figure it out, smart girl.

It was taunting her again. What were these thoughts and where had they come from? Was it true? Did no one love her? Did her own father not love her? Was she a monster? Did she kill Stephen? Phil, why did he want to hurt her? Did she deserve it? What about the baby? Was her baby going to have to live without a father? She heard Gerard's angry voice over and over again, and Guy's, Richard's, Jessie's...Oh God, Oh God. Would anyone be able to save her from herself now?

57.

"She'll be here in five minutes."

Marianne watched the clock in Richard's office. Sarah sat beside her at the meeting table

"Thank you, Marianne."

Richard gathered his files from his desk and took a seat at the top end.

"I didn't invite you both here to gang up on Lillian or to overwhelm her. I want to make that clear. You are both here to open up and talk to her about what's happened. I have you here in *supportive* roles."

Marianne hung her head to avoid meeting Richard's eye. Who was he kidding?

"Marianne, I expect you to behave with integrity. Am I making myself clear?"

"Perfectly."

Lillian walked through the door without knocking. She looked worse than Marianne had imagined.

"Lillian, please take a seat."

Why are they treating me like I'm some kind of psycho? Lillian thought.

"You realise why I have called you here, Lillian?"

What a dick. As if I don't know.

"Yes, Richard."

The sarcasm in her tone angered him. Did she really think she could get away with sarcasm? He thought, furious.

"Before we begin, do you have anything to say for yourself?"

"Yes, I do actually. The reason I'm here is because I tried to rescue an innocent child from a life of sexual, physical and mental abuse. That's my crime."

She was acting righteous.

"No, Lillian. You are here because you neglected the project you were given the responsibility to oversee. You just walked away from it to fulfil your own personal agenda, which, might I add, was as reckless as it was STUPID."

He was raising his voice. Did he really think that was going to scare her?

"I had every intention of returning to Tanh Hoa on time."

"Intention? You know what they say about the road to hell, Lillian. I don't want to hear about *intention*."

"Oh kiss my ass, Richard. You're such a non-entity. The road to hell! What a load of shit. Trust you to speak in outdated, irrelevant *proverbs*. You're a gutless-civil-servant-turned-philanthropist who lives his life vicariously through young people—who have COURAGE. If I were you I'd check your pants to see if your balls are still there."

"How DARE you."

Richard stopped himself finishing his sentence.

Marianne stepped in.

"Lillian, it must be hard being the only one to know everything."

"Don't get me started on you, you victim. Do you have *any* independent thoughts? Or will you *forever* be enslaved by the false idea that sucking rich people's asses—and god knows what else—will get you to where you want to go? Get a clue, you groomed, conditioned, brainless lemming."

Marianne was startled. Sarah fought the urge to cry.

"Lillian, stop, don't say those things."

Sarah pleaded with her eyes for Lillian to stop firing.

"I'm sorry, Sarah. I'm leaving now."

Richard marched her to the door, aflame with indignation.

"Lillian..."

He looked her hard in the eye, forcing her to pay attention to what he was about to say.

"I've been where you are. You're done with it—you don't believe anymore. But, and trust me on this one, you need help. This isn't you. The Lillian I know is a smart, beautiful, ambitious young woman. She has a future ahead of her. Don't destroy that girl."

Lillian's hard front snapped and softened to tears.

"It's all gone to shit."

"I know how that feels," Richard whispered, hugging her close.

"Lillian, I know you're smart enough to know that I have to let you go. I'm not saying that I'll never take you back again but I am saying that, for now, you have to go."

Victoria stopped Lillian on her way through the office.

"Lillian! You were right, about Marianne. She *is* just a brainless lemming. I heard everything. The walls are like paper 'round here. Someone had to say it to her, at last!"

Victoria had gotten too much selfish pleasure out of Lillian's state, and Lillian didn't like it.

"Well it was never going to be you, you gutless little lick arse."

She pushed passed Victoria's locked jaw and left the building.

58.

There was nothing left. No home, no job, no love. What label could she put on her suffering? How could it be emptiness, when inside her nerves had no space to stretch or breathe? When her chest felt so tight it could burst? When a baby was growing there? How could that be emptiness? There was no space, no air.

She was being hammered by her own thoughts. How could anybody understand a person who hurt themselves with such self-generated vitriol?

Her thoughts spun independent of her.

How? How can my thoughts be independent of me?

She had always learned that personal development was about taking responsibility for thoughts. How could she take responsibility for something over which she had no control?

A tornado of painful sensations spun around her temples, ripping at sensitive nerves. Her guts pulled in opposing directions. An excruciating migraine made it hard to open her eyes.

She sat on her suitcase in Liverpool Street Station, waiting for the Piccadilly to Heathrow. She was going home to Ballybeg a failure; a lost, tattered, broken shell of a once happy girl. She was going home to be a single mam.

59.

Time had no significance. Hours passed into days without change. Lillian lay in her childhood room, surrounded by My Little Pony décor, Disney posters, ugly wallpaper and rows of trophies. Her floral curtains had been closed for days.

Nuala was at her wits end.

"Lillian, I think it's time you went to the doctor Flynn."

Nuala used her firm voice and ripped the curtains apart to let in light.

"For the last time, I'm not going to a General Practitioner under the influence of some drug pusher of a pharmaceutical rep who doesn't care about anything but earning money. And anyway, what's Doctor Flynn going to do? Prescribe the latest and greatest brain-altering anti-depressant? I don't need a tablet, I need peace and quiet."

And I'm pregnant.

"Do you understand how serious this is? You don't know everything, Lillian. You don't even know how to look after yourself."

"Please leave me alone."

"Do you know how selfish you're being?"

"SELFISH?"

"Yes, selfish, that you can't see what you're doing to me and your father?"

"My father? Don't bother."

183

"He cares about you."

"He cares about no one."

"I don't know what more I can say."

"Say nothing, nothing is good."

60.

Petula hadn't seen or heard from her best friend in over two years. Lillian had stopped making time for her when she had moved to London, mailing her with excuse after excuse until contact naturally faded out. But Petula would always love her as the girl that set her up for her first kiss; the girl who shared the buzz of wearing her first lipstick outdoors, and the girl who laid with her in summer fields under starry skies, dreaming up the future. No amount of time or space would ever really come between them.

Despite the reassurances of fond memories, the palms of Petula's hands began to sweat as she approached O'Shea's house.

"Petula, love, it's so great to see you. Thank you for coming. She's upstairs."

Petula tried to imagine the condition she would find Lillian in. She couldn't have been as bad as everyone made out.

"Hey, Margaret, are you alive or dead?"

It was Petula; beautiful, crazy, funny Petula.

"Frances, 'tis yourself."

Lillian managed a cheerful salute.

" 'Tis."

Petula made her way to the bed and locked her friend into a hug.

"What's happened?"

"I'm a mess."

"You surely are. Your breath smells like cat piss."

"You never changed. And what is *that* you're wearing? A rainbow dress with red leggings? I should have been here for you."

"And you think you've mastered the London look, do you?"

Lillian acknowledged the quip with a raised eye and changed the course of the conversation. She had surprised herself by being cheery and was ready to return to misery.

"So, dish it. What are they all saying about me?"

"Oh, nothing, just that some salivating beast was seen walking through the village with a suitcase, knocking off polls and small children."

"You cow."

After the quiet laughter, an awkward silence filled the air.

"Lillian, will you talk to me?"

"I don't know what to say."

"Say what you feel."

"Lost, tired, alone, scared..."

"Go on..."

Lillian tried to stop herself crying. No way, she thought, was she crying in front of a friend she hadn't seen in years. Then the choice left her.

"I'm panicked. All of the time. About everything. When I'm not nervous or frightened, I'm scared. Not regular scared: terrified shitless scared. I can't breathe. I'm not comfortable around people. I can't describe it."

Petula understood. Lillian wasn't aware that she had gone through her own dark night; that she had felt the pain of falling to pieces once before too.

"I know what you mean."

"You do?"

"I do."

"But...how? I mean, you're the first person who hasn't looked at me with fear. Everyone else is telling me to be 'positive.' I mean, *come on*, if I was fucking able to be positive, I'd be positive!"

Petula burst into laughter.

"I know. Have you heard that time is a great healer yet?"

Lillian attempted a laugh, which came out as more of a huff.

"I have. And 'there's plenty more fish in the sea', 'you're only young' and 'it's just a broken heart."

"You'd almost wish it on 'em, just so they could know."

"That's a bit dark."

Petula grinned in pride.

"I'm kidding. Maybe just a minor dose."

"Petula, I'm so sorry. I just upped and left you and vanished from your life. I was a rubbish friend."

"You did what you had to do. You're still my girl."

Lillian cried into the raggedy tissue that had turned her nose red.

"Mags, I think you need a new tissue. That one's covered in snot."

Lillian couldn't understand how someone was capable of making her laugh.

"And Mags, you'll get through this."

It was exactly what Lillian needed to hear. And finally, it was from someone who had the authority to say it.

6I.

A gloomy nightscape spread black blood across the forest, making a villain of everything that moved. Lillian was on the highest branch of the mightiest Oak, protected, as a tortured version of her was violently dragged through a shallow river. Phil, the protagonist, acted out the part of barbaric aggressor, pulling her along viciously by her hair, as though his role were to mangle her, crush her—maybe even end her.

The moonlight lit up the screen with the expert discrimination of a spotlight, craftily keeping the peripheries in darkness. Victim Lillian was visible to observer Lillian only by the bright white dress she wore, all torn and bloodied from the bashing against splinted rocks. She was helpless, pathetic; lifeless, as she relinquished resistance to the river's torrent and Phil's cruelty.

She gasped back to full consciousness in a cold sweat, horrified, terrorised. She cried with her hands pressed hard to her face. What was happening to her? What did the dream mean? Was she dying inside?

She had read Carl Jung; about his work on archetypes and their shadows. He believed that archetypes were universal characters in each of our personalities. Different shadow types appeared in intervals throughout our lives, particularly through periods of disturbance or growth. The dream had raised all the red flags.

She figured, amateurishly, that the woman appearing in the dream had to be her Shadow Victim; a personality she had never come face to face with. It terrified her.

It terrified her? She almost laughed at the realisation. She was now afraid of her own shadow, that sorriest of indignities. And as though that weren't pathetic enough, she thought, she was afraid to return to slumber, afraid of a subconscious mind so dark that it spun only reels of horror and torture. What to do but pray for respite from the pain, and wish instead for symbols of hope and peace to float up through the murky cesspits of her disturbed mind.

The mind doesn't work like that, she reminded herself, to which a more dissident part of her replied: *it ought to.*

She returned to sleep full of resistance.

She lay on a stretcher in a dark morgue, alone. She had been left there, by the window, to die. An eyeball hung out of its socket. Her face was draped in bloodied bandages. Her mouth hung agape and salivated.

She woke to the safety of morning's light, sat up and looked at herself in the mirror at the bottom of her bed. She loathed the person in front of it; for her weakness, for her cowardice. Why couldn't she just pull herself together? She walked towards the image and began to beat it, crying desperately for it to change into something she wanted to see. The person looking back at her wasn't loveable. Not to anyone, least of all herself. There was nothing worth living for anymore, and even if there were, she had given up believing she was capable of accepting it. She was a mess, a hopeless Godforsaken mess of a person. If God existed, if there were in fact a mightier power pulling the strings of creation, could he/she/it, she asked; please intervene before she killed herself.

I can't do it alone. Please, God. Please get me out of here. Please tell me what I'm supposed to do. Please. If I've been a bad person, if I've hurt people, I'm sorry. Maybe I deserved this, but please take away this pain. Please, God. Show me the way out of here. Please. Please. Please. I can't do it alone.

She twisted her rigid limbs into the comfort of the foetal position and cried for what could have been; for what should have been. If Stephen were alive, her father would have loved her. They could have been the perfect family. And she would never have had to live with parasitic guilt, with shame, with low self-worth. She would never have settled for security in a relationship over love. Phil, with his big ugly head and zero charm would never have had the chance to cheat on her. She would have been a stronger woman, not a tireless self-doubter.

And if she hadn't gone to Vietnam, if she hadn't entertained romantic, grandiose ideas about saving the world, she would still have a career.

And for fuck sake, she hissed, *if I had just been on the pill, I wouldn't be so fucking pregnant.*

She began to loathe herself for the poor decisions she had made; for risking security for thrills, and for neglecting the only true friend she ever had: Petula. Was she shallow? Had she been deluding herself all her life that she was a good person, when really, deep down inside—in the place where she kept all unsavoury emotions—she was just an insecure, approval-seeking little girl?

Tears burned her eyes as she sobbed in heaves onto her lavender-scented pillow. Nuala had trickled the essential oil on its laced edge so she might sleep better. Her mother believed in the healing properties of lavender like no other and had dripped some in an oil burner beside her bed—to cleanse the room of bleakness—and, very sweetly, on the tissues that were wiping up the slimy residue of her daughter's emotional breakdown.

Lavender was no cure. Sleep offered no pause either, and the long-term effects of psycho-altering drugs, Lillian felt, were too risky. If she swallowed pills, she might as well wave goodbye to her self-esteem, to her self-control and respect. Alcohol would surely tip her over the edge.

Her mind raced to the edge of its boundaries, furiously catapulting her outside her comfort zone.

She walked to the toilet to splash herself with sobering cold water. She sat on the edge of the bath and leaned on the sink. Her anguish exploded in her chest. She begged God for a good reason, for guidance—anything that would show her that there was a purpose to life. She fell to the floor in desperation. The pain gnawed at her.

Please God, she cried out loud as she looked up at wooden penguin chimes hanging from the white ceiling, *Please get me through this.*

After another rejected plea, she returned to her lavender sanctuary, defeated, and pulled the covers over her head. She wanted to die.

Where was her controller now? Where was the voice of reason that pulled her through the hard times? Had even that left her? Was she just a rotting carcass, unappealing even to parts of her own personality? Had her backbone hitched a ride with her controller, as though to signal its opposition to her pitiful state? She had destroyed the environment in which they had thrived. She had starved them of their vital life force, the rudimentary nourishment they relied on for survival. No part of her could muster up the ingredients for happiness, let alone turn them into a positive belief or attitude. She was utterly bankrupt, impoverished and beleaguered as she played unwilling hostess to uninvited guests of darkness.

As she thought analytically for a while about the dark characters of her new personality, she remembered a poem she used to read. She had been captivated by it for some reason, even though it didn't really provoke resonance in her, kind of as though some day it *would* make sense. Maybe her rationale was nothing more than a self-fulfilling prophecy, she thought; or maybe, more positively, it was prescience from a wiser part of her that intuitively knew that life, some day, would challenge her for all she had. Maybe there was a subtle psychic thread running through her ethereal constitution and it understood the importance of committing a poem like it to memory.

Maybe.

She walked to her shelves and picked up the poetry book. Just touching its soft cover lit up something inside. It was her first favourite poetry book, by Rumi, an ancient Sufi poet from the mystical branch of Islam. She lay on her bed with one hand resting between her thighs, the other holding the book close to her eyes, as though to make absorption easier. Of course, she knew it didn't work that way, but there was something about Rumi's words that made her want to be close to them; physically, intellectually, soulfully—any way she could. As she began to read, her eyes softened in comfort.

This being human is a guest house.
Every morning a new arrival.

A joy, a depression, a meanness,
some momentary awareness comes
As an unexpected visitor.

Welcome and entertain them all!
Even if they're a crowd of sorrows,
who violently sweep your house
empty of its furniture,
still treat each guest honorably.
He may be clearing you out
for some new delight.

The dark thought, the shame, the malice,
meet them at the door laughing...

But answer this, Rumi: What happens when demons overpower? There's nothing in your poem to answer that.

Her guests, parasites, burglars—whoever they hell they really were—didn't just knock on her door, they burnt it down with flame throwers and drove through it with steamrollers. They terrorised her, their unwilling host, with a cruelty she never imagined existed.

Meet them at the door laughing? Surely, Rumi was on opium.

But maybe, she thought, there was a chance, however small, that it was a cleansing; a great purging. Maybe she was, as he said, being cleared out for a 'new delight.'

'Yes, her baby. Maybe a baby girl. She drifted back to sleep on the fragile hopes of possibility.

Maybe she could make it all OK.

62.

Nuala sat up in her bed and reached her ear closer to the sound of sobbing to make sure she was hearing it. *Where was it coming from?* She opened the door into the sunlit early-morning corridor and located it in the bathroom.

She walked to the door.

"Let me in, Lillian."

Silence and bird chirps filled the long pause.

"Lillian? Let me in."

She knocked louder and twisted the door knob furiously.

"Go away. Please, just leave me alone."

"What's wrong?"

"Nothing's wrong."

"If you say so, Lillian."

"I do."

Gruesome, terrifying clots of blood had come as messengers. She rocked beneath the sink and held her knees close to her chin.

Why didn't I take better care of myself? she asked, as her tears streamed in a lonely torrent.

Who would want a mother like me?

I would have loved you, baby.

I'm so sorry. I'm so sorry. It was only ever me and you. You're my little secret, baby; my little angel.

I'm so sorry, I'm so sorry.

63.

"Who is it?"

"Petuala."

"Oh."

Petula burst in, stampeding her seven-stone frame across the floor.

"Well woop-dee-do to see you, too."

Lillian shivered at her buoyancy.

"Well, Madam Lillian, will you be talking today?"

"Please, just get out."

"No, I won't actually. You see, I planned a day out for us."

Lillian sent her daggers.

"I have everything we need for a charming picnic: flask of tea, blanket, mother's homemade scones, fruit..."

"Just leave me alone. You're making me angry."

"I don't give a fiddler's fuck *what* I'm making you. Soon enough you'll see that you're the only person making you feel *anything*. But for now, if you want to be angry, then be angry. Who knew you'd turn out like Miss Holiday?"

"Miss Holiday?"

"Ya, that's what I said."

"Really?"

"Yes, really."

Miss Holiday was a cantankerous old woman who lived alone in a cottage on the edge of Ballybeg. She would snatch up all balls that had the misfortune of bouncing into the parameters of her weedy, overgrown garden. It was one of life's funny ironies that her surname was Holiday. The woman was permanently imprisoned by her distorted beliefs about the world and the people in it. She never had a holiday in her life.

"You don't have a fucking clue. I don't *want* to be an angry, bitter person. I'm *locked in*, Petula. You don't know the half of it. You don't fucking get it. "

"I do get it. Now get over yourself and get dressed. You look like shit."

"Thanks."

"You're welcome. Now *go*, get dressed."

"Fuck you."

"Pardon me?"

"I said: fuck you."

"Lillian..."

Petula sat on the edge of the bed and rubbed her hands up and down her friend's trembling back.

"...What is it? What's wrong? You're so angry. It's not like you."

Lillian curled her knees under her chin and clasped her hands together. She tried to speak over her tears.

"I was pregnant, Petula."

Petula's eyes widened behind her friend's back. Her soft, composed voice concealed her shock.

"When?"

"Until a few hours ago."

Petula put her hand to her mouth and held in her tears.

"I'm so sorry, Lillian. I'm so sorry for coming in like this. I just, I thought it might do you...I'm so sorry."

"Don't be. I brought it on myself."

"Don't say that. Come on."

Petula took off her shoes after a long period of silence and curled in beside her friend.

64.

Autumn slowly surrendered herself to winter. Pat weeded out her dying flowers, trying to let her go. He was attached to the red leaved months in a way he couldn't put into words or thought. He relied on others to do that sort of thing for him, and when it came to autumn, it was John Keats. Fall, as the poet articulated it, was the season of mists and mellow fruitfulness; a time when passions were tempered, fevours were cooled and people were happy to be. Even the fieriest sidelined their hyper talk about diets and holidays and festivals. The warmest chill filled the air, the kind that made people calm.

The temperature was still moderate enough for Nuala to recline in her woollies on a striped patio chair. Pat toiled the soil beside her, enjoying the comforting exchange that could only happen when they didn't speak.

Petula and Lillian emerged from the double doors of the conservatory onto the patio, Lillian in an unseasonal temper. As Petula walked past Pat, she complimented his gardening skills, unable to resist an opportunity to melt a frosty moment. Pat didn't reply.

"Are you really that ignorant? She's talking to you."

"Hello, Petula."

Pat ignored Lillian's anger, submitting instead by returning a late greeting.

"What's you're problem with me? Say it. Come on, strap on a pair and tell me what your problem is."

Anxiety turned Pat's mouth to sand.

"I have no problem, Lillian."

"You're a sorry excuse for a father, do you know that?"

Nuala sat up nervously in her chair. Pat responded calmly, despite the adrenaline pumping through his every atom.

"Is that so, Lillian?"

"Yes, it is. You can't even look at me. You wish it was me, don't you? All these years, you've been wishing it was me and not him. ADMIT IT."

"Lillian, stop it."

Nuala never thought the words would be spoken.

Pat stood up, trowel in hand, and faced her.

"Sometimes, when you behave like this, I do."

He had just ripped her guts out.

65.

She hated him with every last fibre of her being.

How dare he! How dare he say those cruel things. I don't deserve it.

What choice did she have but to speak out; to let him know how she had always felt? Avoidance had become pointless. Avoidance had brought on a meltdown; a miscarriage. Avoidance was the cause of her life's problems.

What cruel karmic controller had mapped out this life story for her? Why did she have to endure the men in her life? Why the hell could no one love her the way she wanted to be loved?

Whys streamed in endless whirlpools, leading her deeper into her self-created void.

She willed herself to find her centre.

If you don't stop what you're doing, you'll end up where you're going.

After a second's reflection, she was hijacked by her gnarly compulsion to self-sabotage.

No one can love you. You're all alone. You will always be all alone. You can't depend on other people for love. Learn this, FOR PETE'S SAKE. Get it right in your twisted brain that life just works that way. The world is a cold, dreary, miserable place to be. Forget about the purity of unconditional love. It does not exist.

She didn't want to believe it. She didn't want to believe in a world where people didn't love unconditionally.

A parent's love: surely that's unconditional?

No, it's not. Your father doesn't love you. What more does he need to do to get the message across to you, stupid? Quit your desperate search for love and accept that you won't find it.

She held her palms to her face and cried with a temper that made her shoulders heave.

No, No Way. No *way*

There was no way she giving up her faith in pure love.

NONE.

She'd sooner die of gout. Whatever cruel circumstance tried to throttle her, she would fight back.

Fight back, Lillian.

A determination, a determinator, scrapped its way past her weak tormentor. Her mind had spawned a new partner. She was prepared to fight with it for her beliefs. There *was* such a thing as pure love.

Transmuted, she walked with her new accomplice all the way home, feeding it affirmation after affirmation. She would prove that she was loveable, that she was loveable.

Nuala met her at the door.

"Lillian, I've never been as worried in all my life."

She looked wearied.

"You know your father didn't mean what he said, don't you?"

She had softened, turned desperate, and needed Lillian to give some her a sign she understood.

"I don't need him."

Nuala pulled on her arm, stopping her escaping through the kitchen door.

"You don't need him?"

"You heard me. Now please let me go."

"Lillian, I'm begging you. Please sit down and talk to me. For me. For my sake, not yours."

It was impossible to reject her; a woman who was desperate enough to believe that lavender could fix things.

"Fine."

"We'll sit outside. I've the outdoor heater on. I'll brew some chamomile tea, get you nice and relaxed."

Chamomile tea, Lillian thought flatly, *that ought to make things right.*

She played with the string of the teabag, avoiding her mother's overly concerned eyes. She loathed pity.

"Why did you bring me out here?"

Nuala paused for a moment.

"Lillian, you're father hasn't been right since Stephen. You know that."

"No way, are you serious?"

"Don't be snappy. Let me talk to you."

"Alright. Fine."

"He rejected counselling back then. He rejected God, too—and any other form of help to get him through. No man can digest that alone. Lillian, can't you see that the guilt is eating him alive? He honestly believes that he doesn't deserve to heal."

"Maybe he doesn't."

"Watch your mouth. I know you're hurting so I'll pretend I didn't hear that."

"Sorry."

"Just know in your heart that I love you and *I know* your father loves you, too. Darling, please have the vision to see that it's not *you*."

Nuala held her daughter's sunken chin in her hand, pleading with her to find the strength.

"He has so much pain inside that he just can't see yours."

Lillian kept her eyes down as they spilled the tears of her torture.

"He must have done something great to deserve a wonderful advocate like you, mom."

Lillian tried to collect herself, to stifle the surge of erupting passion.

"But tell me this: who's going to advocate for *me*? Are you going to ask him to sit out on the patio, make him a nice cup of tea, and urge him to see that I said those things because of my *pain*? Are you going to ask him to be a better person? Are you going to ask him to love me, warts and all?"

She looked her mother square in the eye.

"You know as well as I do that approach wouldn't work."

204

"I do. And I know this, too: the only thing he will *ever* communicate with on any *meaningful* level is Stephen's memory. He's in the shed right now, isn't he? Playing with Stephen's train set."

"He probably is, Lillian."

Nuala answered calmly, inviting her daughter to see how innocent it really was.

"He's in there loving a ghost when I'm out here ALIVE. Look, see— there's blood in these veins."

Lillian stood up and thumped the insides of her arm.

Nuala tried to pacify her daughter with silence.

"I'm dead to him."

"Sweetheart, you're not…"

"No more. I can't do this anymore. Sometimes I think you're as bad as each other."

66.

He got his first tooth at just three months. They didn't know what was wrong. Lillian had always been so easy. But not Stephen; Stephen was different. Nuala had almost pulled her hair out. They thought there was something fatally wrong with him. Like the stereotype of panicky new parents, they considered a trip to the hospital. But fortunately for their respective self-images, they decided to ride it out until morning, when they saw the tip of his very first tooth had broken through. He smiled as he lay between them in their bed, kicking his soft, chubby little legs into the air. Nuala had taken Lillian shopping to buy him one of those silly 'My First Tooth' boxes.

The pain swallowed him, engulfed him; broke him. His baby boy really did die like that, on the road, in a pool of blood. What would have been his last thought? Would he have wondered where his daddy was? Would he have wondered why they let this happen to him? Would he have been afraid? What? What would he have thought?

It ate at him. It extinguished his hope. As he looked at the train set in front of him, he thought back to Stephen's last Christmas and tortured himself a while longer.

67.

The picnic had been hijacked by their tragic argument. Petula longed to pull Lillian out of the quicksand. After her own journey to rock bottom, she had found purpose in healing; perhaps as a way to pay the gift of healing forward.

On Petula's lowest day, when she had heard suicide exchange words with a weaker part of herself, an angel walked into her life. Jane was how she had introduced herself; the name she gave to her human form. She was a Homeopath by qualification, with short summery hair, little legs and a lilting Irish accent.

Petula's mother had suggested she see her after 'some woman' recommended her. She still thanked God for that acquaintance of her mothers. The kind stranger was a minor stitch on the golden karmic thread that had weaved the tapestry of her redemption, but an essential one, like the kind in time that saves nine. For that, Petula would forever be grateful to the woman she didn't know.

The day Petula met Jane had been a grey Tuesday. She had suffered a panic/sorrow/terror attack in the shower. Afterward, she sat into the passenger seat of her mother's car to go and meet the 'might-as-well-try-her' woman. Her mother waited outside while she knocked on the door beneath the red canopy, as instructed.

She had been nervous, unsure of what lay ahead. After the buzzing noise—and what she interpreted as a serious tone—she was invited inside to climb the narrow stairway to the clinic. She, the oracle, had on a hand-woven scarf, expertly swept over her thin frame, which looked at home beside her turquoise earrings. The moonstone ring finished the signature Healing Goddess look.

No one had ever spoken to her the way Jane had. No one had ever led her to the core of herself as gently. And no one had ever asked her to replace analytical judgements with simple words.

Jane wasn't interested in stories; she was interested in sensations, feelings, energy. She wanted to know how Petula felt inside. The hows and whys seemed unimportant to her, yet still she was able to direct Petula to answers she has searched for her entire life.

After a few sessions, Petula began to see life's bigger picture. She trusted herself to unlock the door of her self-imposed prison and go outside to enjoy limitless freedom and peace. It was her birthright. Joy was her birthright. What a fresh approach. And her fears? They were never any realer than the thoughts in her head. It was that simple. She found the courage to let it be that simple.

Jane introduced her to the healing properties of water. Imagine, Petula had gasped, that life could be made easier by *water*?

It was no flimsy assertion by a flaky woman, Petula understood at the time. Jane was backed up her statements with proof from the research on water crystals carried out by a Japanese scientist, Dr Masaru Emoto.

"He, a bearded, spectacle-wearing scientist, collected water from Fuji Mountain in Petri dishes," Jane gently explained.

"He wasn't exploring its molecular structure or mineral content; he was testing for magic, and magic he found."

Jane lit as she spoke the words.

"This is what he did,' she had said, as though she were revealing the secret of the universe.

"He invited a Buddhist Zen monk to bless one of his water samples—he had a hunch that it would alter the basic nature of the water, which turned out to be true. Because after the blessing; when he returned the water to its place under a powerful magnifying lens, the composition of the crystals had changed from average to resplendent."

She made her words clear for the novice in front of her, whose open-mouthed look of awe could have been mistaken for stupidity.

"When water is magnified to sub-atomic levels, images of crystals appear. Yeah?"

Petula nodded an affirmative.

"The water reacted to the monk's thought, Petula."

She looked at Petula's vacant expression.

"When Dr Emoto asked a second person to say the word 'No', the crystals turned ugly and amorphous...

...So don't you think there's a chance that we create our own reality, our environment, with our thoughts?"

"I suppose...there's a case for it."

In the aftermath of her sessions with Jane, Petula navigated her way through the mysterious field of Quantum Physics, chewing up mind-healing concepts like Relativity, the Observer Effect and the phenomenon of Discontinuity. Physicists had proven that the way we see the world is not how the world actually *is*.

How is it in reality?

The question burned inside her.

More than that question, she wanted to understand her truest essence. The answer eluded her. She grew desperate to experience her 'Absolute Self'—the boundless Self described by the gurus and seers of ancient India.

She shelved fond memories and entered Lillian's room to find her buried beneath an avalanche of blankets.

"Lillian, are you awake?"

It was late in the morning.

"Lillian, I know you're hurting now. I know you feel like you want to die; that the whole world is against you; that no one gets you. But you're wrong. I'm going to very cheeky here and tell you something. Are you able to hear it?"

Lillian was numb. There was nothing she couldn't hear after what she had heard her father speak, after what her own subconscious mind had done to her. After losing her baby.

"Try me."

"This suffering, this pain you're clinging so tightly to; can I put it to you that it's your ego."

"My EGO! How dare you?"

Lillian sat up in the bed, horrified at her friend's assertions, which she considered shockingly wide of the mark.

"You're saying that a lot, Lillian. Listen to me, I may not be putting it right, but I know someone brilliant who can convey the truth of existence to you in simple words."

"The truth of existence? Petula, come on. Mankind hasn't yet found conclusive proof about THE TRUTH OF EXISTENCE. Honestly. You won't tease me out of this condition."

"I'm not teasing."

"I don't get you."

"You will. Trust me."

Petula reached into her wicker basket and handed Lillian two books: The Power of Now and A New Earth, both by Eckhart Tolle.

"And these are going to reveal the mystery of life to me?"

"Quite franky, Lillian, yes."

"You're madder than you are insensitive."

"Au contraire, mon ami. You're the one lying in bed on the last of autumn's beautiful days, feeling suicidal, when *just outside*, there's a blue sky and a meadow waiting to be basked in. You've completely lost your ability to be present in the moment. You live in your head 24/7."

"I still don't get you."

"Just promise me you'll read the book."

"I'll try."

"Don't try, do."

68.

Lillian's mind blared on full volume, noising out the theatrical performances of cruel voices. She had cut Petula's picnic short; complaining of a headache, which might have ended up true had she stayed listening any longer. Why did people who didn't understand her feel obliged to say they did? It was wrong, plain wrong, she boomed.

Having had enough arguments in her recent history, Lillian chose not to confront her last friend

As if Petula knows about loss or guilt or grief.

Her father loves her, dotes on her.

Back in her room, where colours clashed as loudly as the thoughts in her head, she slumped onto the bed and threw the books across the room. She was angry at what Petula said they represented.

If it were that easy, Petula thought, she would have been saved by the million other books she had read in her lifetime. It was insulting. Despite her anger, she grew curious.

Imagine, her thoughts whispered to her, *that in just reading a few lousy words, you'll find your way out of this hell. Try it. Do it! What do you have left to lose?*

A surge of crippling pain kicked-in before she could respond to her thought's request. She tossed the books aside, sat on the edge of her bed and cried.

She remembered the good times with Phil, how he had once loved her, how he used to call her princess. Sometimes, he would run baths and fill them with banana bath bombs. And when she was engrossed in research at her desk, he would sweep the hair from her face. He was the only person in the world able to make her believe that nothing bad would ever happen to her again.

What had she done to make him take it all away?

She thought back a few years to their first break up. She did it, and had almost felt powerful in a twisted way she wasn't entirely willing to admit.

"I'm just not in love with you anymore."

He had fallen to his knees, cried like a baby. She felt no remorse, only a sense of power. How twisted and sordid was that? she thought, ashamed of herself.

"It's really not about you. I have to find myself. I need room to grow."

It was straight out of Dawson's Creek. After a month of separation, she had enough of sorting out her own problems. He accepted her back with open arms. A year later, almost to the hour, she dumped again.

"It's not you, it's me. I'm confused. I don't know what I want."

Regret attacked her, made her pay for what she had done. It was time to pick up her karmic tab, to repay the debt she owed.

She could understand that bill-flouting was punishable but why, she asked, did she have to lose everything *at once*? Why couldn't they—the faceless string pullers—allow her to make a *series* of repayments? Why was she learning the whopper lesson of the century? Why did she have to lose her job, her relationship and her hope in some day having a loving relationship with her father in *one lousy month*? Why did she have to lose her baby?

Anger was her meanest emotion, but one better than guilt. It spat out righteous monologues in quick succession. Diatribe after diatribe, Lillian convinced herself that it was all wrong, that none of it should have happened to *her*. She had tried to be a good person her whole life. She had.

Anger was the policeman that guarded the boundaries of her sorrow, never allowing wisdom to shine its light in. Anger watched over her most fragile emotions; it protected and promoted her self-image. It was important to have it around.

In return for its protection, anger demanded a takeover of her physical wellbeing; freedom to boil blood and ruin peace. Above all else, love perished when anger was around.

I do want love, she assured herself.

But anger was so powerful.

She was always right when it was around.

69.

Nuala sat in the conservatory watching bronze leaves float away from tired branches. A plume of smoke appeared in the distance, past the trees at the bottom of the garden.

Probably the Sheridan's burning dead foliage.

The open window let in crisp air, turning her nose effervescent. She closed her eyes and breathed deeply, trying to forget for a moment her worst nightmare was playing out in reality.

Thoughts interfered.

What in God's name could she possibly do to make it right? At times, she wanted to choke Pat for being so stubborn, so blind. Why was he intent on punishing himself? Why couldn't he let Stephen rest in peace?

If her little boy was looking down on them now, and she was sure he was, he would hate to see what had become of them.

Nuala had read everything in publication on the afterlife and had stitched the major teachings of each book together in her mind. All souls were karmically bonded in this life, she had come to understand; and they chose to live certain lives with specific people so that they could learn spiritual lessons. Grace came in many different forms, she had also learned, and sometimes it came in the form of excruciating pain. For her, it had come to pull her home, back to where it was known that she was a soul in a human body. Were it not for her grief, she would not have searched for truth. She accepted after many years of anguish that she had chosen this life, where she would suffer the loss of her child.

Souls were immortal and lived many lives until they reached self-realisation. It was a journey, a cycle, an eternal pay of creation to which she would forever be part. Love was the glue that kept it all together. Stephen was merely on the other side of a veil, in another dimension. Her gross mortality, encaged in human form, could not access him there, at least not until death. But Stephen could access her. She felt him around her. She felt it the night he came to her in a dream, smiling sweetly and waving to her, to let her know he was alright, to stop hurting.

Awareness was the spark that lit up life-experience and it did not need form to exist. Awareness was everything.

Pat entered through the aluminium conservatory door where Nuala was.

"I didn't hear you come in last night."

Her voice was soft, indifferent.

"It was late. I went to the pub."

"And this morning? You were gone before I woke."

"I gave a hand with Willy's calf."

"Oh."

"I got some mince for the dinner."

"You know she doesn't eat meat. And I'm trying to accommodate her right now, Pat. You *know* that."

"I'll get on with my own dinner then. Ye pair can have what suits ye."

"Pat," Nuala called out as she turned around to face him, "this all has to stop. Do you hear me? I won't put up with it any more. Not under this roof."

Pat returned to the house without responding.

70.

Lillian lay on her bed and stared out the window. Her eyes focused on virtual situations in her mind.

"LILLIAN," her mother shouted down the hall, "PHONE."

"Who is it?' she thought, vaguely curious, half afraid."

She made her way down the hall corridor, catching the stench of fried meat on her way.

That man is such a barbarian.

"Hello?"

"Lillian, so good to hear your voice."

Deepa.

"I don't believe it! How are you?"

"Great. Hey, you forgot to say goodbye."

"I know. I'm sorry, I was...I *am*, all over the place."

"I understand."

Do you though?

"Listen, the reason I called: I'm leading a retreat in Wicklow this weekend. Is that close to where you live?"

Lillian's heart beat faster.

"Yes."

"Great! Can we meet? I'm staying at a hotel close to, how to say this... Glen-da-loog?"

"*Glendalough.* Oh, right. Well...yes. Yeah, why not? Text me the details. I'll turn my UK phone on."

"Do, please! I had to do a lot of sucking up to get your home number— to *Victoria*."

The name sent chills through Lillian.

"Oh, right. Sorry about that."

"Well, I'll be in Glendalough in a few days. Can't wait to catch up."

"Yeah, me too."

Lillian dropped the phone and smiled. Nuala saw it as she passed by with a basket of laundry.

"Good news, Lillian?"

"Kind of..."

"That's wonderful."

"Yeah, I suppose."

"Dahl for dinner tonight?"

It was sweet of her mother to pretend she knew about vegetarian cooking.

"That'd be really nice, mam."

"Brilliant!"

Nuala beamed all the way to her whirlpool washing machine.

71.

Lillian plugged her phone charger into the wall and shivered.

What if there are messages I don't want to see?
What if I can't stop reading them?

What if Phil has sent some?

Or worse, he hasn't?

Twenty three new messages.

She opened her inbox and scrolled through the messages. Jessie, Sarah, Scott...She searched for his name. Not there. Not one lousy message.

Surely, she thought, *he's emailed me.*

She patiently waited for the internet to connect to her parents' old PC.

Four hundred new messages. None from Phil. When she was unable to convince herself any longer that she had missed it, she let her heart sink.

The lousy bastard didn't spare a single thought for me. All those years and not one message. He has no fucking heart, no soul. I always knew it.

It's my own fault for going out with him in the first place—someone with a fucking calculator for a personality.

How had she tied herself to someone so shallow? she asked herself; a person who wanted to live out a carbon copy of a conventional married life.

He was probably already in a serious relationship, she prophesised, convincing himself he had found the one; when really, deep down, all he wanted was someone to make pregnant and buy a house with.

If only he knew how close he was to having it with me; the conniving, heartless bastard.

HOW DARE HE!

Anger was back, fuelling her every loaded thought. She stormed to her room and slammed the door. She was RIGHT! About EVERYTHING.

Nuala cocked her ear out from the laundry room.

What was all the racket about? Surely, she thought to herself, Lillian hadn't done a U Turn already?

She sighed long and hard into her bumper box of Persil.

Would she ever get a break?

72.

Deepa breathed in the emerald landscape around her as she strolled along a quiet country road; past stone walls and flowery cottages, up to the V-shaped valley at Glendalough. Inside its entrance, an ancient round tower spiked out from an old graveyard. Ruins of churches lay peppered over the sacred site.

The earth beneath her whispered peace. She walked towards the Upper Lake at the end of the meandering river the guidebook said resembled rosary beads.

She stared into the autumn forest on the way; at its grassy floor and spiralling branches. A few steps up the trek, a gushing mountain river crescendoed into a foamy white waterfall, stealing a gasp from her. The forest, as she saw it, twinkled charm.

She arranged to meet Lillian at the visitor's centre at noon, minutes away. As she turned back she spotted her friend's lofty frame standing by the flag masts. Lillian had the hood of her rain jacket up and had on red wellingtons. Deepa hadn't perceived the weather as brutal.

She walked to her silently, sending her healing vibrations all the way. Positive thoughts emitted positive energy, she knew well; and her friend looked in need of positive energy.

Lillian walked into Deepa's hug silently. There was something about her friend's presence that made her feel calm, at ease with herself.

"I'm so glad you're here. It was rude of me to ask you to go on a retreat with me, and then leave you in the lurch. I'm sorry."

Deepa smiled at her.

"Nonsense. I wasn't mad at you, I was worried about you. Are you alright?"

"I'm OK; sometimes. I guess. I'm just having a...I dunno, crisis of some kind. It's all just empty. Life means nothing, except pain."

Deepa paused on her friend's words before responding.

"I think we should go back to the hotel and have lunch. *Then*, come back here for a healing session? It's the perfect place for it."

"Healing session?"

"Yes, if you're willing?"

"Can't hurt."

"I admire you're willingness to explore, Lillian."

Lillian felt shy at the compliment.

"Thanks, I think."

Deepa laughed and patted her friend on the back as she led her down the road to the nearest village.

"It's all going to be just fine, Lillian. It's already fine."

Lillian looked at her, perplexed and curious.

Already fine? She thought. *How does she figure that?*

73.

Pat felt a lecture coming. He had ignored Lillian at the breakfast table. *The Irish Times* must have been more important, Nuala had said afterwards. It was hard to face up to what he had said which, naturally, he hadn't meant. Guilt, the peskiest of his pests, had started to nibble his insides.

"Pat, she doesn't know you like I know you. She can't read your mind the way I can. You're hurting her."

"I know."

"Then for God's sake, will you *do* something about it?"

"She's not totally innocent here, Nuala."

His wife let the saucepan plop into the suddy water. She threw her eyes to the heavens.

"Yes, pat. She *is*. She's the *most* innocent person here."

"How do you figure that?"

She took off her yellow marigold gloves and turned to face him, leaning one hand on the wooden countertop.

"Because her father, through his *inability* to communicate, made her feel her whole life that it was her fault her brother died. Because *in the middle of an emotional breakdown* he told her he wished she were dead. Do you want me to go on, Pat?"

His legs stretched long in front of him as he leaned back in his rocking chair beside the range. His arms were folded.

"Are you actually falling asleep while I'm talking to you?"

"Will you ever give me a break, Nuala?"

"That's all I give you, Pat. But tell me this: when am I going to get MINE?"

She torpedoed through the kitchen door out of sight, leaving him alone with the thorn in his side. Had he really made Lillian feel like it was her fault?

74.

"Just let the rock take your weight. Let go of all resistance. Know that you're safe."

Deepa's kind voice allowed Lillian to relax on the blanket on the floor of the forest.

"Close your eyes and take a deep breath in...a deep breath out."

Lillian focused on the air moving to the bottom of her lungs. Her breaths were shallow, then deep and consoling. She listened to the rain drip-dropping over crispy branches, the river in the distance, and the tweet of the remaining birds. The air was fresh, enchanting, transporting; heavenly.

"Remain focused on your breathing."

Lillian withdrew her attention from without to within where, to her surprise, all was quiet.

"Keep your eyes closed and trust."

Deepa whispered at her to spread her limbs wide, to sink naturally into the earth. Lillian's body vibrated, as though magnetised and seeking out its polarity deep inside the earth. She sank down and down.

Deepa moved her hands in rhythms over her friend's distressed energy field, focusing on her Solar Plexus, her Manipura: seat of power and contentment.

Lillian felt her navel heating up. On the screen of her mind, a bright light sparkled into life; yellow, growing brighter and brighter. A forgotten feeling bubbled inside, like joy, but in a form purer than she had experienced. She stayed with the feeling until it faded. Deepa wiped her eyes and blew her nose.

"That never usually happens," she smiled.

Lillian opened her eyes and sat up on her elbows.

"What *was* that?"

"A mixture of different energy healing techniques. Did you enjoy it?"

Deepa smiled, anticipating the answer.

"*Yes.*"

Deepa answered Lillian's flood of questions as they walked through misty rain back to the hotel.

At a small mahogany table beside a stone fireplace, over cups of hot chocolate, the conversation deepened.

"Just remember," Deepa said to Lillian, "that thoughts are as real as this table in front of you. Without thought, it would not exist. The outside world is entirely dependent on mind."

Lillian knew this, having read widely about the laws of the universe on Jessie's recommendation.

"Yes, I know—like the law of attraction..."

Need she go on? she asked her friend with a raised eyebrow

"Exactly,' Deepa smiled. "But remember, that's just the phenomenal world."

"The phenomenal world?"

"Yes, the phenomenal world, where things *appear* to happen. It's all really nothing more than a grand illusion, a dream. The Indian scriptures refer to it as Maya. What you are, in essence, lies far beyond what you see with those blind human eyes."

Deepa laughed as she wiped cream from her top lip.

"Is that a bit much?" she asked Lillian.

"A bit, maybe. Let's take baby steps."

75.

Lillian looked up at the grey, gloomy clouds and felt understood. Barely able to contain the tears that wanted to burst out of her, she waved goodbye to Deepa, presently the greatest comforter in her life.

She walked to her mother's car, turned the ignition and waved to her friend, whose golden complexion lit up the pale environment around her.

Thank you, Deepa. Thank you, thank you, thank you.

She turned the car radio off and held her attention on her 'inner energy field,' as Deepa had suggested. She had also mentioned Eckhart Tolle, whom Petula kept quoting in their conversation. Maybe the universe was giving her a sign, she thought.

76.

"You're back! I missed you."

Petula smelled of buns and cream.

"Been baking?"

"Indeedy. Nicola's birthday tonight—coming?"

The thought of a social engagement repulsed Lillian.

"No, thank you."

"Not to worry. Come in, you'll have tea."

Petula led the way to the kitchen, where her father was lounging by the fire, just the way her own father did. He walked towards her and kissed her on the cheek.

"Lovely to see you again, Lilly. Been a long time!"

"You too, Paul. Really nice to see you."

Lillian bowed her head and wondered if Paul knew about what was going on with her. Petula sensed her tension and invited her to the living room.

"Great idea. Why don't ye two ladies go inside and I'll bring ye in a nice cup of tea."

"To share?"

"Don't be so cheeky, you little brat. CUPS of tea—plural."

"Thanks, dad."

Petula laughed as she rolled her eyes.

Lillian burst into tears as the huge mahogany door closed behind her.

"What's wrong?"

"Oh, nothing. I'm fine."

"You're not fine. Just talk."

"It's. . .it's my dad. I know I sound twelve but, *really*, I hate him."

"Not true."

Petula stroked her friend's back.

"It *is* true. You were there. You heard what he said."

Fugitive mucous spilled from Lillian's nose.

"I'll get you a tissue."

"He didn't mean what he said, Lillian. You were quite aggressive with him that day."

"I know, but. . ."

"No but. You *were* and he snapped."

"But it's been all my life, Petula; not just lately."

"I know it feels to you that he doesn't love you, because yes, you're right; he's never shown it. But consider that his inability to show love is not a reflection on you being a loveable person."

She always spoke sense. It was almost annoying to Lillian, who felt like indulging herself.

"I know, but it's hard. It's really hard."

"I can imagine. But you're strong enough to get through this. If it's meant to be resolved then it will be resolved. And it will. Every argument spins itself out in the end."

Lillian listened on absently in vague belief.

"Why won't the pain just fuck off and leave me alone?"

Petula burst into laughter.

"Lillian, it will, as you say 'fuck off' when you stop thinking it has more power than you, that it's stronger than you are."

"But it is."

"And there's you're problem. Surrender to it and see what happens. Just surrender, Lillian."

"Ladies!"

Petula's dad peeked in the door, using his foot to push it open.

"Two cups of Paul's special with extra marshmallows!"

"Marshmallows in tea?"

"In *hot chocolate*. My special."

"But we asked for. . .never mind. Thanks, dad."

Lillian wiped her eyes and avoided Paul's.

Can't he just fall over?

77.

"So, like, why is a 26-year-old *ambitious* woman like you still living at home with her parents?"

Petula had always disliked Paul, the prettiest of all the jocks at school. She was certain that an ego of his size could never see that life wasn't about a gargantuan bank balance. And she was wise enough to know it was unwise to tell him the real answer: that she was happier working as a waitress than as a career orientated stress bitch, as she had once intended.

"I guess because she's happy to."

Petula let him dent her ego. Because, really, the situation was nothing more than an opportunity to see she still had one.

"Oh. Right."

Paul looked at the starch-collared guy beside him and drank down the bottom of his pint. The deliberately indiscreet grin that followed was intended to diminish her.

As if you have the power, Petula laughed to herself.

"See ya later, Paul."

In the past, comments like his brought out the fighter in her. Now, she allowed the old energy to spin out, like a wheel no one was pushing anymore. She didn't need to defend her life choices to anyone, least of all a veritable cognitive moron.

She walked to her sister Nicola, who was writhing around with older men, daring them to have fun; poking them out of the mundane hypnosis that was guiding their lives further and further into ordinariness.

Her sister Nicola was freshness incarnate, wearing a huge lemon flower headband in her fusilli-curled red hair. A blue polka dot shirt with shoulder pads and pink skinny jeans could only look good on her, Petula thought, proud.

"Petula Petal. Come on, dance with me!"

Petula ignored the stares of the wives at the bar; the unfortunate victims of early-onset rigour mortis.

Lighten up, she wished she had the nerve to tell them.

Only Nicola, Petula thought, could make Honky Tonk music fun. A song later, they plonked onto a large couch and caught their breaths.

"So, tell me: how's life? As in, really," Nicola asked Petula.

"Great."

"Even though you're living with mam and dad?"

"Yes, *even though* I'm still living with mam and dad. What is this place? First Paul, now you?"

"Hmmm...do you want to move to Dublin? You could stay with me until you got yourself sorted."

"Thanks, Nikki. But I'm no rat-racer."

"I know, but life's *better* there. There's always something on, places to go, things to see..."

"Listen, and I mean this respectfully: I just don't need constant stimulation anymore. I'm happier with less."

Nicola pursed her lip, confused.

"Are you sure you're not depressed?"

Petula smiled.

"Yes. I'm sure I'm not depressed. So thanks, but no thanks."

"If you say so."

"I do."

"So, how's Lillian? Dad was saying she's had a bit of a..."

"She's going through a hard time, yeah."

"Right."

"But she'll pull through. And when she does, she'll see that contentment is causeless."

"Ever the philosopher, our Petula. But come on, everything depends on something."

"It doesn't have to."

"It does so. D'ya want a drink?"

"Birthday champagne?"

"Of course. And you're not going to tell me that champagne doesn't cause happiness."

78.

Lillian lay on her bed following her breath and trying not to think. There was a knock on her door. It was him.

What does he want? she thought, angered by his imposition.

"Can I come in?"

"...O...K?"

He walked in without looking around and sat as far outside the reach of the lamp's light as he could. A pointless action, Lillian thought, since his behemoth frame made his disappearance impossible. His big feet were wrapped in tattered slippers, his white shirt unbuttoned at the collar.

"Are you well?"

What do you think?

"Yeah."

"That's good."

Is it?

The silence held until Pat mustered the nerve to do what he had come to do.

"The other week; what I said to you in the garden. It wasn't...about..."

Lillian watched on, struck, as his voice quivered awkwardly.

Why is he doing this?

"I didn't mean what I said...I just..."

The words grated against her.

"Don't bother, dad."

"Pardon me?"

Pat looked at her from his dark corner.

"I said: don't bother."

"But you don't know what I was going to say."

"I don't, but I know *why* you were going to say it. Mam sent you."

Pat stood up.

"She didn't..."

"She did, now get out of my room, please. This is awkward, and totally unnecessary."

"But I was only trying to..."

"I said STOP. You don't get to step in after all these years. I don't need you. I'm all grown up now.'

Lillian walked to the door and held it open for him.

"It doesn't look that way to me."

"How dare you," she screamed. "How dare you come in, uninvited, and tell *me* that *I'm* the undeveloped person in the room."

"I didn't…"

"GET OUT."

Pat paused; stopped himself saying what he was about to, and walked through the door.

"And don't come back."

He tried another sentence from the hall.

"Lillian, I shouldn't have said that. It was wrong."

"You shouldn't have said, *or done*, a lot of things. But you did. And you just have to live with that. How *dare* you walk in here with that half-arsed apology and expect me to meet you with open arms."

"Please, Lillian. Stop and listen to me. It's not easy for me."

"For *you!* Do you think it's easy for *me?*"

Pat looked at her, exhausted, defeated; sorry.

"Please, just give me a chance. That's all I'm asking."

Lillian let the silence hang.

I can't do it, she thought. *I can't forgive him.*

"…I find it hard to talk about these things."

"Dad,' she said, sternly, making sure she caught his eye, "I don't care. Now, please, just go. I don't want you."

Lillian slammed the door closed.

79.

He had gone straight to the shed like the coward he was. Lillian tossed and turned in peacelessness. Had she really said those awful things? My God, he was just a man; he hurt like anyone else. Stephen was his son.

Tell him you're sorry.

Oh my God, look who's back? The Controller!

Find him and tell him you're sorry.

Lillian put on her robe and slippers, picked up a torch from the conservatory and made her way to the shed. As she traipsed over stones and rocks, hitting her barely clad big toe on the edge of one, she cursed him.

I shouldn't have to worry about him. He should be worrying about me. This isn't right. It's all wrong.

She opened the door, mid-ramble, and dropped the torch onto the floor. In the faint light of the moon, she could see him; really see him, for the first time. She stood frozen, watching his massive back as it trembled. She recognised the force was moving him as the same one that clawed her guts. The pain was inside in him, too. It was the most natural ache in the world, and one his own daughter, *Me*, Lillian whispered in guilt, couldn't allow him.

He turned slowly, aware that he had blown his cover; aware now that his daughter could see him at his most flawed; most human.

"...It was *my* fault, Lillian. Not yours. Don't ever think for a second that it was your fault."

His agony haunted her.

"Not yours."

Lillian's lips curled as she tried to restrain herself.

"Do you hear me? *I* was supposed to pick you both up that day. You were just a child. Ye were too young to be walking that road alone."

He buried his face in his hands.

"Why have you never spoken to me about this before?"

Lillian's voice was sturdy. A spontaneous wave of strength supported her.

"Any why did you make me feel so bad? You had to know what you did to me. You can't pretend you didn't see me suffer. Dad, I pissed myself every night until I was fourteen."

"Lillian, I'm sorry. I'm not perfect."

"No, you're not."

"I don't expect you to understand me. Christ, I don't understand myself. But believe me: you could *never* understand the guilt I've been carrying all these years."

"I bet I could."

He turned his head around and looked at her in shame.

"We've had our darkest day, Lillian. Nothing can hurt us the way we've been hurt. We share that much. But the pain will get worse for me if…"

"If what?

"…if I lose another child."

Lillian wanted to run to him, to throw her arms around him. She approached him, guarded, and rested her shivering hand on his shoulder. His aged face crumbled in his hands.

"Don't do this, dad. Don't carry all of this guilt. I *forgive* you, dad. But not for that day..."

She paused to stop herself crying; to finish the most important sentence of her life.

"I forgive you for all the days that came after; for taking your love away, for leaving me alone in pain; for making me feel like I was unlovable. I know it wasn't my fault. I know that now, dad, as an adult. But I didn't know it then. And I suffered. I suffered more than a child should have to suffer."

She took a moment's pause before delivering the words of both their redemption.

"It wasn't your fault that he died, or mine. It just...it happened, and there's nothing you or I could have done to change it."

Pat moved his shaking hand onto hers.

"He's missing, Lillian. He's always missing."

"No, dad. He's here, he's always here."

80.

"Ahhhhhhhhhhhhhhhhhh. Shoo! Shoo! Go away! Get lost!"

"Ahhhhhhhhhhhhhhhhhhh."

Lillian leaped from her bed, pulled back the curtains and laughed until her guts tickled.

"Paaaaaaaaaaaaaaaat! Shoo! Shoo! Ahhhhhhhhhhhhhh"

Nuala ran in circles, poking a wayward chicken with the yard brush. Pat ran to her and picked the chicken up.

" 'Tis only a little chicken, Nuala. Look—he's more frightened than you are."

"Don't start on me now, Pat. I swear, I'll hit you a wallop with the brush. Just get it out of here."

Lillian ran down stairs and out to the circus.

"He's right, mam, it's just a lickle chicken."

Lillian tried to coax her mother into seeing its harmlessness.

"Don't you start too, Lillian. PAT! I said get that chicken out of my garden. I bet it's the Sheridans. I swear, I'll have words with Mary when I see her next."

"And what will you say, mam? That her *killer* chickens are on the loose?"

Pat erupted into laughter.

"We'll have to call neighbourhood watch, too—to report a break in."

Pat and Lillian cackled at his joke as Nuala backed towards the house.

"To hell with ye. Go and fuck off."

Lillian's eyes stretched in shock. Pat hooted in uncontrollable laughter.

"We're in trouble now, Lillian."

"My God, she's gone mad!"

"I can still hear you," Nuala shouted from the conservatory.

Lillian covered her mouth with her hands and looked at her father, who was holding an index finger to his.

"Not another word, Nuala. We won't say another word."

81.

"That's really wonderful. Wow, finally."

Petula smiled as she rubbed Lillian's arm.

"I know."

"Let's get some lunch."

Lillian stopped at the gate outside her house to check the post box. Her blood ran cold. It was Phil's writing, on a purple envelope.

"Everything OK? Lillian?"

"Am...it's....it's Phil. He's written me, a...letter."

"Oh. Right. I'll leave you to it."

"No. Please. Don't. Read it to me."

"Here? Now?"

"Inside, upstairs."

Dear Lillian,

I've been racking my brains trying to find the perfect words to make all of this right. I'm a mess without you. She meant nothing...'

"Stop right there, Petula."

"But it goes on for another...' she scanned the pages, front and back, '*Eight* pages."

"Here, give it to me."

Lillian balled the paper up and threw it in Petula's bag.

"Throw that into the fire when you get home."

"Will do."

Silence. After a few minutes, Petula spoke.

"Are you not curious? Don't you think it'll give you closure."

"No, Petula, I don't. I got my closure the second I caught him in bed with that *whore.*"

Lillian's anger ripped through the space between them.

"Don't let him set you back."

"He already has, the *prick*. And just when I was feeing stronger."

"There'll always be something to get you down, if you want there to be."

"Sorry, Petula? If I *want* there to be? Do you think I *want* this?"

"Have you read the books yet?"

"No, and why are you so obsessed with them?"

Petula laughed softy.

"I'm leaving now, and you're going to read them."

Petula picked up the books from the floor on her way out and tossed them at Lillian's side.

"And when you do, we'll talk."

Lillian shouted at the closed door and threw the books at the wall.

82.

Dissipation, evaporation, melting away, knocking down, bulldozing through. The Controller's empire had fallen. The thoughts were gone, like the wisps of air they were. They were all self-created. Her problems were *self-created*. How could it be that *simple?* Why was it so clear now? She flew out of her body and the prison of her mind in one swoop. One. The scope of her consciousness became boundless. In pure awareness, she burst through the ceiling of her room, out over the village and up into space, the solar system, the universe. Lightness rushed through her heart like water from a mountain stream. Love was its current and as it bubbled through her, it tickled enlightenment out of its long, long slumber.

Freedom, I'm achieving freedom. Right now.

She returned to gross reality for the final burning. The rusting chains that had been strangling her guts burst apart in a massive explosion. A huge earthquake erupted in sudden realisation that *she was not insane.* Someone out there knew exactly what was happening to her and how to free her.

Where has this man been all of my life? My God, this is what a man should be.

Her problems could be boiled down to one. Just one. And this *one* problem did not include Stephen's death, her issues with her father, losing the baby, her job, or even Phil. It was about addiction. Addiction and, identification with, thinking. The Controller? Its rogue opponents, all of them, had nothing to do with who she really was. The nightmares, the dreams, the dread.

How had she become so *addicted* to thinking? The book had blown her brains out.

Page 18. The Power of Now: A guide to spiritual enlightenment.

'*Because you are identified with it (thinking), which means you derive your sense of self from the content and activity of your mind. Because you believe that you would cease to be if you stopped thinking. As you grow up, you form a mental image of who you are, based on your personal and cultural conditioning. We may call this phantom self the ego.*'

It explained so much; so much about the sudden split inside her after Vietnam, the strange voices in her head. Instinctually, in the core of her gut, she had known the thoughts and voices weren't her own, that they were somehow independent of her. But she couldn't shake them. Why? *Because modern personal development has taught me to take responsibility for myself.* To Lillian, that had always meant taking responsibility for *thoughts*. No wonder she had begun to feel imprisoned by her growing neuroticism and anxiety. She was resigning herself to a life of slavery, having given up on trying to control the feral behaviour of *thoughts*. What a major, groundbreaking, startling, beautiful revelation—she was *not* her thoughts.

Page 13. She took out a pen and paper.

'*The mind is a superb instrument if used rightly. Used wrongly, however, it becomes very destructive. To put it more accurately, it is not so much that you use your mind wrongly—you usually don't use it at all. It uses you. This is the disease. You believe that you are your mind. This is the delusion. The instrument has taken you over.*'

A process unfolded inside. As thoughts streamed in, one after another, they puffed, crackled and snapped into nothingness. They were not her, they were not to be believed or taken seriously. Thoughts, she could now see, were nothing greater than the manifestations of a single mechanical function of the body's mind—thinking. And, most importantly, she was not the thinker. She was the awareness that noticed the thought. Thinking was just another function of the body that she did not control, similar to digestion and circulation. Satre had come close to pointing to this in his work on existentialism, which she had read in college, but was too caught up with thinking to get space from it. Now, thanks to Eckhart, she could see.

My God, this is huge. This is really huge.

248

She could feel it; a spaciousness freeing up the constricted cells of her body. An insatiable hunger for truth arose. Who was she, really? Beyond positive thinking and mind management, who was she? What was the most authentic part of her?

Page 14. More hope; more beautiful, glorious hope.

'The moment you start watching the thinker, a higher level of consciousness becomes activated. You then begin to realize that there is a vast realm of intelligence beyond thought, that thought is only a tiny aspect of that intelligence...You begin to awaken.'

She stood back from her thinking, listening objectively to its mad murmurings. It was true: her thoughts really had *nothing whatsoever* to do with her. Why all the suffering? Was the author really saying that life could be entirely free of pain and sorrow?

Page 27. Yes.

'The greater part of human pain is unnecessary. It is self-created as long as the unobserved mind runs your life. The pain that you create now is always some form of unconscious resistance to what is. On the level of thoughts, the resistance is some form of negativity. The intensity of the pain depends on the degree of resistance to the present moment, and this in turn depends on how strongly you are identified with your mind. The mind always seeks to deny the Now and to escape from it. In other words, the more you are identified with your mind, the more you suffer. Or you may put it like this: the more you are able to honour and accept the Now, the more you are free of pain, of suffering—and free of the egoic mind.'

But why did she have to go through so much pain? Why had it been so intense?

Page 29. Because she had been unconscious her whole life.

'Every emotional pain that you experience leaves behind a residue of pain that lives on in you. It merges with the pain from the past , which was already there, and becomes lodged in your mind and body. This, of course, includes the pain you suffered as a child...'

Page 30. Pain is a beast.

'*This accumulated pain is a negative energy field that occupies body and mind. If you look on it as an invisible entity in its own right, you are getting quite close to the truth. It's the emotional 'pain- body.'*'

A thought entered her mind; a 'what if?' thought. What *if* the mind tricked her into identifying with it again? How would she make sure it could never trick her again?

It was already doing it.

Page 31. Bring in the light.

'*The pain-body, which is the dark shadow cast by the ego, is actually afraid of the light of your consciousness. It is afraid of being found out. Its survival depends on your uncon- scious identification with it, as well as on your unconscious fear of facing the pain that lives in you. But if you don't face it, if you don't bring the light of your consciousness into the pain, you will be forced to relive it again and again.*'

83.

The cold rain started to bucket as Lillian took off on what had become a daily early-morning stroll. At this time of the year, it meant one thing: the beginning of a long and miserable winter. But Lillian had never felt happier, more at peace, more alive and one with the whole world. Everything was fresh; the rain, the grass, the sky, the earth. She had never seen nature this way before; never smelled its fragrance, or tasted its fruit. She had never *felt* it this way before. Without thoughts, her eyes were free to see the world in front of her. Her attention was free to feel the life in her body.

"Nothing exists except that which is truly natural. Thoughts have no reality in and of themselves. They are not to be believed." The realisations breezed through her.

A New Earth. Page 26.

'Even a stone, and more easily a flower or a bird, could show you the way back to God, to the Source, to yourself. . .When you don't cover up the world with words and labels, a sense of the miraculous returns to your life. . .The quicker you are in attaching verbal or mental labels to things, people, or situations, the more shallow and lifeless your reality becomes. . .Words reduce reality to something the human mind can grasp, which isn't very much. Language consists of basic sounds. . .Do you believe some combination of such basic sounds could ever explain who you are, or the ultimate purpose of the universe, or even what a tree of a stone is in its depth?'

She sat beneath a spiralling labyrinth of leafy branches under a huge Oak tree. As she nestled into a comfortable seat on the earth, she focused on the life, the force, the energy, moving through the tree; keeping it alive, blooming, ever-changing. She imagined the complex circuitry of roots and channels beneath the earth; the vast networks supplying crucial nourishment to its vital organs, all the way to the leaves at its peripheries. It was blossoming in total perfection. *Total perfection.* She could feel the life in the tree. She could feel magic. Pouring rain saturated its tired, fading leaves, creating U-shaped troughs at their centre.

They overflowed in gentle cascades, inviting the leaves below to join the dance. All around, there was pure, exquisite, playful beauty.

> 'To the ego, the present moment hardly exists. Only past and future are considered important. This total reversal of the truth accounts for the fact that in the ego mode the mind is so dysfunctional...Identification with your mind comes between you and nature'

She watched panicked adults drag confused children along the nearby road, and smiled. It was true. The thoughts in their head were telling them to run; that they would get drenched, soaked, die of the flu. The mild rain was causing no-one harm. It was the *aversion* to the rain that was causing harm. Resistance to nature, Lillian could now see, was endemic.

What an illness, what a collective mental illness.

84.

The same frenzied passion that took over new lovers had spread into Lillian's every cell. She couldn't bear to be apart from nature. Wonderful, beautiful nature was all she would ever need. Feeling this alive was all she would ever need. She rose at first light and walked to the estuary at the Southern tip of the town; a routine she had been keeping for days: nature, food, more nature, sleep.

This morning, over the glistening river, the sun flirted with the ether, appearing in sporadic bursts through the clouds. On a royal green carpet, miniscule clusters of sparkling rainbow light twirled along the peaks of the grass's thin blades, subtly introducing their majesty to those with the eyes to see. Lillian understood that she was witnessing nature's dawn ritual; a sacred and playful dance of the great elements. Deep feelings of gratitude pervaded her inner body. Casting her blue eyes skywards, she watched brilliant golden clouds in a light blue sky. One by one, their wispy forms took turns rolling past the rising sun. She felt waves of soothing energy rain down on her, raising her vibration higher and higher. It was her first experience of natural bliss.

A solitary bench at the river's edge invited her to take a front-row seat. The water's perfect stillness created a glass mirror, doubling the span of the sky's beauty. Everywhere she looked, she could see divinity. Taking a seat, she gave her attention to the water amusements. The same breeze that was folding the water into tiny ripples was the same breeze blowing her blonde curls. She began to feel a deep sense of unity with everything outside of herself. She felt her boundaries thinning and allowed herself to just be; to let her breath move to its own natural rhythm. She noticed the gaps between each soft, slow cycle. A personality-shaking epiphany spontaneously arose within her: theses gaps were the bridges to her soul, the doorway into her being. Being was found in perfect stillness. She understood that now. This morning had changed her. She was never going to believe another thought again. Everything she ever needed had always been and would always be. True reality, she was seeing clearly, had been missing in her life.

Lightness took over her entire form, tickling vibrations of natural joy into movement. The all-pervasive, delicate sensations intensified in her legs. *This is what drugs must feel like,* she thought. *This is the feeling people chase after.* She felt privileged to see things from this rare vantage point; for the new vision that gave her eyes to see things from this beautiful, peaceful perspective. Bending her neck back, her sight was arrested by the patterns of wispy cirrus clouds in the sky, doodled onto the brilliant backdrop of the sky by the brilliant stroke of nature's magic wand. The words of Rumi's poem danced to the front of her consciousness; *yes,* she thought, *the pain was clearing me out for some new delight.*

A floating dandelion twirled above her face, turning round and round as it danced with the breeze. It settled on her shoulder, where she watched as it tried to free itself from the woollen fibres of her sweater. Stephen's laugh began to ring in her air. The dandelion game they used to play. *My God,* she thought, *I remember.*

Outside their garden gate, where weeds and daisies and dandelions grew, was where, Stephen would say, the lions slept. Dandelions became lions at night. Sometimes he would scare himself so much with his wild imaginings about lions eating him in his sleep that he wouldn't go to bed at night. To make him feel safe, Lillian would take him outside and blow the fluffy flowers until there was nothing but the rod left. Stephen would get great consolation from this and would laugh and play with the feathery remains of the flower as they blew in the air.

A tear streamed down Lillian's cheek as she listened to the memory of Stephen's laugh. A calm sort of grief enveloped her, a vulnerability so beautiful it didn't create aversion. As she smiled at the memory, she tenderly picked the dandelion from her sweater, held it in the valley of both her hands and blew it gently into the sky.

Goodbye, Stephen. My heart is always with you.

85.

"You look different."

Petula approached Lillian tentatively, taking a seat at the edge of the conservatory sofa.

"I feel different."

"Has it happened?"

"Has what happened?"

"You know; enlightenment?"

Lillian observed a light, tickling sensation in her stomach and the movement of her mouth as it laughed.

"Nah, but I'd say I'm closer to it than I've ever been, put it that way."

"Was it Eckhart?"

"Yes, it was Eckhart."

Petula reached for her friend and wrapped her arms around her.

"I *knew* you'd get it. I *knew* you would!"

"Where has this knowledge been all my life?"

More laughter, more bubbling sensations.

"You know what Eckhart says?"

"What?"

"That you can only become open to spiritual teachings when you've had enough suffering; that only when the ego starts to become insufferable will you search for the truth. Obviously, Lillian, you had enough suffering."

"I can't dispute that."

"Let's celebrate. Let's go out and play. Ooo, I know—let's go with Nicola to her boyfriend's football match later."

"Sport?"

"Don't discriminate. Athletes are people too."

"I didn't mean..."

"I know, just say you'll come. We'll have fun."

"I'll come."

"Yay. Pick you up at seven."

"I'll be here."

86.

"When you said you'd be here I didn't think you'd literally still be here."

"She hasn't moved from that spot all day, Petula. She's just been staring out at those trees."

Pat smiled as he nodded in Lillian's direction.

"Trees are beautiful, what can I say? I've never really seen them before."

"Don't be saying those kind of things around your mother."

"Don't worry dad, you don't need to worry about me anymore."

"Get ready, Lillian—we need to leave," Petula said, moving her head towards Nicola's parked car.

"I'll just get my coat."

"But, we're going out after for a few drinks after the match. Don't you want to put some…*nice* clothes on?"

"I'm fine as I am."

Lillian rose from her seat gracefully and smiled, assuring her friend there was nothing to fuss about.

"This is new."

"Yes, it is."

Lillian sat into the back of the Mini Cooper and smiled as Nicola attempted a sympathetic greeting through the rear view mirror.

"You don't have to tiptoe. I'm fine, Nicki. Really, I am."

"Alright then. Am...so...like, are you on the pull?"

Petula thumped Nicola's arm.

"Ouch, what the fuck was that for?"

"She's just out of a relationship. You know that."

"Petula, it's fine. Maybe I am on the pull, who knows? What does this town have on offer?"

"Wahey! That's the Lillian we know and Love. There *are* some hotties around these parts, I can tell ya now—don't be listening to little Miss Nun Petula. In fact, I've picked up one of my own."

"The way you commodify men is disgusting," Petula butted in.

"Ah, shut up. I was talking to Lillian. So, *Lillian*, as I was saying..."

Nicola's excited chattering eventually reached a point where she didn't need anyone else's participation, giving Petula and Lillian a chance to tune out. Lillian reclined in the back seat; her head pressed to the window, and watched the rain smattering against the pane. She stared at the rain drops with eyes that were lenses of a telescope. Tiny air bubbles within the rain drops bumped shoulders with other miniscule air bubbles. Some air bubbles surged to the surface of bubbles. Some rain drops slid down the window as solemnly as tear drops. Lillian could feel bubbles move inside her. She could feel involuntary smiling, happiness; innocence. Everything in the world was a part of her. She could see it. Her waters moved in reaction to the rain.

All of life is related. All of life is one.

The energy of the football crowd passed through Lillian's unguarded body. In an out, in and out, like her breath. She clung to nothing, no movement, referee's whistle, shout, sensation or tingle. Everything came and went, passing through her unimpeded.

"Lillian, you remember Paul."

Paul's masculine frame captivated Lillian's attention. She felt lightness swirling around her chest.

"I sure do. I kissed him once."

Paul blushed as Nicola and Petula burst into laughter.

"That's right!" Petula screeched, "For about twenty seconds at one of those teenage discos they used to throw us."

"I'd say it was more like ten," Paul smiled, his eyes searching the ground for a distraction.

"What are you doing after the game?" Nicola asked him flirtatiously.

"The pub, I suppose."

"Great, we'll see you there."

87.

"He's still an eejit, Nicola—you realise that?"

"Why is he an eejit?"

"Because he's full of himself. I met him last week and he was all like 'why are you living at home with your parents, Petula. And I was like 'and why are you such a dick, Paul?"

"You wouldn't happen to be judging him there now, would you?"

Nicola looked Petula in the eye; daring her to contradict the belief system she spent her time espousing.

"Because, you know, judgement is unconscious behaviour?"

Petula smiled.

"So you do listen to me."

"Sometimes."

"Right, my mouth's shut. I just, I can't believe they're getting so...so..."

"Spit it out!"

"Well, snug."

"The chemistry is ablaze, I have to say."

"I *know*. I'm so...surprised. I wouldn't have thought Lillian would go for a guy like that."

"A guy like that? You're doing it again, Petula."

"What? I'm doing what again?"

"J-U-D"

"You don't have to bloody spell it. I know what I'm doing, which I'm not actually doing. I'm just saying."

"You're tripping over yourself there, love. Drink?"

"Yes."

"Why are you back home, then?" Paul asked. He couldn't meet Lillian's eyes and played with the beer mat on the counter in front of them to spend his nervous energy.

"I don't really know how to answer that without making you feel so awkward you'd want to walk away."

Paul turned, met her eyes and said: "You're not the shoe bomber, are you?"

Lillian whipped her head back and laughed from the pit of her stomach. Then she turned serious, forcing him to fall for her mock mood.

"Paul, the bombs are I have to make people listen. You people give me no choice."

"Still, though, exploding us is hardly the answer."

The one-time teenage couple burst out laughing, relaxing into lighter and lighter conversation. As one drink turned into four, Lillian couldn't help but like how Paul had started to intermittently rest his hand on her thigh, pretending he needed it for leverage to reach his drink across the bar counter.

At midnight, her girly tingles were interrupted by Petula, Nicola and Nicola's new boyfriend.

"Petula just did a rudy—a dirty Guinness twister fart!"

Nicola's drunk, laughing head fell onto her boyfriend's shoulder—who barely noticed he was winking so obviously at Paul.

"I'm not even going to challenge you on that one, Nicola."

"Ahhhhhhhh, you big fart face. Ahhhhhhhhhhh."

"Hey, Tom Selleck," Petula shouted to Nicola's older boyfriend who had oddly shaped hair growing on his face—and who wouldn't stop staring at Paul and Lillian, "we need to go home. Are you coming too, Lillian?"

Lillian looked at Paul, who answered for her.

"I can take her home. I mean, we practically live next door."

Petula bent in to kiss Lillian goodnight.

"Call me tomorrow so, yeah?"

"Of course. Night night."

Mwah.

After they'd gone, Lillian and Paul moved their stools closer and ordered a round of Baby Guinness.

"Here's to hot neighbours who come home at just the right time."

Lillian smirked, flattered and delighted at his comment, and drank down her shot. As she moved her wincing face from the glass, Paul moved in, put his hand to the side of her face and asked for her permission to kiss her.

"I wondered how long it'd take you to ask," she laughed.

As they leaned in and kissed each other delicately, an eruption of whistling and jeering came from Paul's friends' corner.

"Let's get out of here."

Lillian smiled as she watched Paul call the local one-man taxi. They spoke little on the way home, Paul feeling obliged to small-talk with the town's only taxi driver. As she got out of the cab, Paul touched her arm.

"Come away with me."

"Pardon me?"

Lillian was momentarily frightened that he was about to expose himself as a weirdo. Paul read her eyes and laughed as her reassured her.

"Not *away* away, just a little trip. Just let me take you on a romantic break."

"Where?"

The taxi driver filled the long pause that followed.

"Doolin. He'll take you to Doolin. County Clare."

Lillian and Paul screeched into laugher as Lillian moved to close the door.

"Alright. Doolin it is."

88.

"Because he's so nice and lovely."

"I'm hearing things: I asked you why you're going away with a guy you barely know."

"And I answered your question."

"Alright then. I surrender."

"Surrender is good. I recommend surrender."

"So, what do ye guys have in common? What did ye talk about last night?"

"Life, death, the point of existence, you know, the normal stuff."

Petula smiled and hugged Lillian.

"I'm so happy for you. I'm so happy you're happy."

"I'm happy you're happy for me."

"What's all this happy talk?"

Nuala burst into the bedroom with folded towels.

"Hi mam, I meant to tell you: I'm going away this evening with Paul.

"Oooooooo," Nuala sang, winking at Petula, "she's going away with the new man already. It must be love."

"Mam!"

"Ah, we're just teasing. That's great. Where are ye going?

89.

The Rambler's Inn stood over a spectacular cliffscape on the majestic deep blue water of the winter Atlantic. From the couple's fire-lit cosy bedroom, they could hear the branches of barren Oak trees knocking against the window.

"This is so Cathy and Heathcliff," Lillian said as she lay on the bed next to Paul, enjoying the pleasure of his roving fingertips.

"You're really beautiful, do you know that?"

Lillian smiled shyly.

"I used to think you were the best looking guy in school. Did you know that?"

"The truth cometh out! Then why did you ignore me after our kiss. Hmm?"

"Because..."

"Because?"

Lillian giggled innocently.

"Because I was *shy*. You should have pursued *me*."

"I wish I had."

Paul held Lillian's chin and locked her into his most passionate yet kiss, softly and slowly moving his hands up her loose shirt, over her pink lace bra. Lillian cringed quietly, wishing she had worn a more demure one, and wondered why she didn't think far enough ahead to imagine this scenario. Her thoughts were killed by the arousing sound of Paul's heavy breathing as he moved on top of her, driving himself between her jeaned legs. He tenderly undid the buttons of her shirt and kissed her collar bone. Making his way downwards, he lifted her bra over her breasts and sucked her nipples, using his fingers to rub gently around them. Then he stopped himself abruptly, and apologised. "I'm sorry, Lillian. I got carried away. I didn't take you here to do this. I want to get to know you."

Lillian put her index finger to his lips and took off his t-shirt. His sculpted athlete's body instantly made her wetter. She waited in excitement as he pulled down his jeans and hers. Without foreplay he drove himself inside her, moving in and out animalistically.

"I'm sorry, I can't slow down," he said, licking her ears and moving his stubbly face over her soft cheeks. "And you're so wet you're dripping."

Lillian urged him to keep pushing it in fast and hard with moans and deep breaths, moving his hand over her spot. They continued hard and fast, oblivious to the headboard beating loudly against the paper thin walls. After climaxing, Paul rolled over and laughed.

"I hope we don't meet whoever's next door at the breakfast table."

90.

They crunched the dying leaves with their footsteps outside the hotel. Lillian noticed a heart-shaped twig and beamed. She held Paul's gloved hand tighter as they walked from the hotel path onto an empty beach.

Paul laid out a towel he brought from the hotel room onto the sand.

"Really? A towel?" Lillian laughed.

"Only the best for you."

Paul sat down and tapped the empty spot beside him.

"Come."

Lillian moved to sit down beside him but he interrupted her.

"No, sit in front of me so I can come in behind you and wrap around you, make you warm."

Lillian obeyed, gushing butterflies. He kissed her ear from behind and spoke softly.

"I'm not going to weird you out by saying something stupid, but I am going to say this is the best it's ever been at the beginning of a…"

He stopped himself after realising what he was about to say.

"The beginning of a what?" Lillian asked, in a voice that made it clear she wanted him to finish the sentence.

"Relationship," he said, his lips pressed against her hair.

"Are you asking me out, Paul?" Lillian said, turning around to face him.

"Ah..." Paul's colour drained from his face as he searched Lillian's face for reassurance, which she gave him with a gentle smile.

"...Yes. I reckon I am."

"I just have one condition: you have to be able to accept my politics—when people need bombing, they need bombing."

Lillian giggled, forcing Paul flat against the sand. She laid her head on his chest and laughed as he reacted to her joke.

Enlightenment? she thought to herself, *maybe not, but love—definitely.*

THE END.